For Vivienne
& Michael
with immense
amounts
affection,
Richard

D1827502

Goodbye Europe

Also by Richard de Combray

ATTITUDES ESPAGNOLES,
in collaboration with Michel Del Castillo*

VENICE, FRAIL BARRIER

CARAVANSARY

GIORGIO ARMANI†

* Published in France
† Published in Italy

GOODBYE EUROPE

A Novel in Six Parts

Richard de Combray

Doubleday & Company, Inc.
Garden City, New York *1983*

Library of Congress Cataloging in Publication Data

de Combray, Richard.
    Goodbye Europe.

    I. Title.
PS3554.E11147G6   1983   813'54
ISBN 0-385-18097-7
Library of Congress Catalog Card Number: 82–45122

Copyright © 1983 by Richard de Combray

All Rights Reserved
Printed in the United States of America

for Gini Alhadeff,
Miles Morgan, and
Don Gonzales

Contents

Goodbye Europe

BY WAY OF INTRODUCTION:
Colette

We went there, each of us for our own reasons, though reasons never turn out to be quite as private or original as we hope they will be. Going to Europe, for all of us, meant getting away. And getting away in the fifties usually meant Paris.

It was during that time that I sat one day on an uncomfortable but picturesque metal chair in the Jardin des Tuileries trying hard to read the newspaper without help from my hip-pocket dictionary. The headlines were three or four inches high: COLETTE EST MORTE, they said, and there were photographs everywhere of the beautiful elderly writer, her head half concealed by the thick foliage of curls that framed her face. The eyes, I remember, were remarkable, for after her long, eventful life they seemed to have grasped a final, balanced view, putting the entire matter to rest. Surrounded by the banalities of newsprint and advertisements, their kohl-rimmed wisdom seemed as emblematic to me of Paris as the more concrete and familiar monuments we had all come there to see. I was little more than a kid then. Paris was all of Europe synthesized into one wise, arrogant city, and we foreigners took whatever chunks of it we could pry loose, stayed until our money ran out, and returned home speaking of it, as many of us still do, with a combination of awed irritation and bliss. Clip clop, as a friend of mine says, went the years, about ten of them, and, now a grownup, I was spending a few days on Capri during the summer.

I was living in Rome then. Certain late afternoons in my spare time I would sit in the studio of a friend of mine, a fine sculptor, while he toiled away on a larger-than-life study of my head. Two castings of it were being exhibited in Italy that summer. One of them was on the town square of Spoleto, and its twin, so to speak, was being displayed just off the piazzetta in Capri. It was a heroic-looking bronze, part of an art show conceived that summer by the new center-left government to coat that festive isle with culture.

At first excited by this monumental image of myself, I quickly grew intimidated by it, taking the slender back alleys of the town to avoid running into the great shining thing bristling publicly in the sunlight. On one of these detours I saw in the distance a stocky woman coming toward me with an aristocratic trudge. Her walk was so purposeful that she seemed unwilling or unable to budge either to the right or to the left in the narrow space so that we might peaceably pass. As she neared me she glanced up from a determined study of the path beneath her feet; her eyes narrowed, and at the very last second when we might have collided, she said, "*Aha! C'est vous!*"

Surprised by this unsolicited comment, I began to answer wryly that yes, it was indeed me.

"Tiberius himself," she interrupted, "would not have exhibited such an immense likeness of himself in the town square."

"It was not my doing," I said stiffly. "It's an art show.

The fact that it is me," I added, summoning all the arrogance good manners would allow, "is incidental."

"Even so," she snorted, only half convinced. "It is the second time I've run into it. First in Spoleto near the Duomo and now here . . . Soon, it would seem, the entire peninsula will be packed with them."

Her deep, unruffled voice betrayed a trace of humor, but I would not let her off that easily. We were now filling up the width of the alley, she in her khaki trousers and polo shirt—obviously a resident—and me in a visitor's sandals and shorts. I folded my arms in my then defiant way, locking my hands under my biceps to make them appear more substantial. "I'm not going to apologize to you, madam, just because I am a visitor, either for the bronze head or . . ."

". . . or not making way for me in this alley," she concluded. "No, you are quite right not to." She brushed her gaze past me. "*Look* at that astonishing butterfly!" A smile curved her small bow-like lips and she eased past me to trudge after it as it wound down the road.

By the careful calligraphy of the lips, the retroussé line of the nose, the eternal Frenchness of her as she cried "*Regardez!*," is it only in memory that I sensed who she resembled?

On Capri's main square the clock tower and the town hall receive the last rays of the sun laterally, their shadows stretching gradually across the tables of the Gran Caffè Vuotto, and its cooled seats are instantly occupied. On the steps of the adjacent cathedral young *Capresi* perch as though on bleachers to watch the tourists gather as swallows circle overhead. Shunned now, the sun retreats hastily into the Mediterranean, and only the dome of Santo Stefano re-

turns its paling rays. The atmosphere of the island is
gently halved into the dusk's wistful melancholy and the
evening's bright promise.

I had planned to meet a group of friends at the caffè and
found them all assembled at a table, with two extra chairs
turned down, one of them presumably for me. I righted it
and sat amid greetings, and when I was about to ask who
our other guest might be, I looked up to see coming toward us the same stocky woman I had encountered earlier
on the narrow street.

"*Aha!*" I could not resist. "*C'est vous!*"

Her eyebrows shot up and then she laughed. She extended her hand. "Forgiven?" she asked.

"Forgiven," I answered.

"This is Colette," someone was saying as she eased herself into a seat. *Colette*, I repeated, my mind suddenly
filling with the images of cats and countrysides, and photographs of Colette herself merging with this unexpected
person who, I now realized, so strongly resembled the
writer. Conveniently reading my mind, the companion to
my right mumbled, "*Cretino*. It's her daughter."

"Well!" began Colette to all of us, plumping her hands
against her khaki-clad knees. "I've finally discovered that
the property line between my house in Anacapri and my
neighbor's house is not what they have claimed."

"So you will sue," said someone, as though not for the
first time.

She shrugged, lighting a cigarette to dramatize her presence. "Yes, I shall probably sue." She said this with evident
pleasure, sitting back, completely at home on the piazzetta,
as though the square and Capri itself were her territory.
Later, when we all trooped up to Anacapri, she stopped
briefly at the door of a small restaurant, calling to its pro-

prietor. "I want you to do a splendid *cernia* this evening. You know, with some wild thyme, and a bit of lemon peel. I'll be by with friends around eight-thirty or nine."

"We know, *signora*," he said bowing. "We know. *Stia tranquilla*, put your mind at ease. The fish will be perfect."

"*Mi raccomando*, I'm counting on it," she cautioned. "Among others, there will be an American, and you might as well show off for him."

Our roles in each other's lives, that moment, were sealed: Colette de Jouvenel, who was the quintessential European, emphatically at home—as I would come to know—wherever she found herself on the Continent. And, no matter how long I stayed, or what jobs, friends, places would keep me there, I was, and would remain the foreigner.

It was an uneasy truce. I cannot say that over the years we became friends, for friendship implies a closeness we could not manage, though we saw each other periodically and always had a good time. The first visit I made to 9 rue de Beaujolais had the inescapable aura of a pilgrimage.

A stone plaque was attached to the façade of the Palais-Royal next to the mezzanine floor: "In this house COLETTE lived from 1927 to 1929 and from 1938 until her death on August 3, 1954." So many of the twentieth-century pre-war wonders swirled around me as I mounted the dark staircase: Proust's comment that he loved walking about in Colette's brain; Cocteau's description of her, a fox terrier in skirts. She had inhabited the full mosaic of Paris from her scandalous performances at the Moulin Rouge to her election as president of the Académie Goncourt, a Paris before my time and immeasurably seductive.

Inside the apartment it was as I had hoped. I found the red room, the "raft" on which she wrote, reclining; the luminous collection of paperweights, and, here and there, framed butterflies. Colette watched over my camouflaged investigations with a practiced eye, a matronly "Bel-Gazou," as she had been called in memoirs, surrounded by— and keeper of—these historical things. And so, tourist and native, we talked, avoiding the ever-present subject of her mother, for the daughter's historical burden, I felt, had always been a mixed blessing, and once again we were sitting opposite each other in the late afternoon. The sun slanted across the quiet, secretive arcades, filled long ago with bustling cafés, where Sainte-Beuve and Lamartine dined at the Grand Véfour. And burnishing the leaf tips of the gardens beyond the window, the last light evoked images of Desmoulins announcing to an astonished crowd that within a day or two there would be a revolution that would change the world.

She served a terrine of duck on the desk (her mother's?), pushing aside a thick pile of correspondence. I praised the pâté and the cool glass of wine.

Colette eyed her accomplishment with skepticism. *"Oui,"* she conceded, stretching it out, *"Ça peut aller . . ."* It will do. Measured praise, always, the particular sense that whatever was achieved was expected, and no more.

"Well, I think it's great," I said with contradictory enthusiasm.

"Not to diminish your compliment," she said. "But one of the things Americans do that bewilders me is the way they hand around superlatives. Present company, as you say, excluded."

"The French are more doubtful," I said. "At heart everyone is a concierge. Present company excepted, of course."

She smiled. "More discerning," she said after reflection.

Then, through some circular logic, she added, "Diderot, over one hundred years ago, wrote the opening sentence of a novel with 'Fine weather or foul, I go most evenings, around five o'clock, and walk in the gardens'"—and here she gestured briefly toward the window—"'of the Palais-Royal. I am the person you will find daydreaming, alone . . .' I can't remember the rest. What I mean to say is that it is now about five o'clock, and the gardens are still there, and someone is surely wandering through them daydreaming . . ." She faltered.

". . . and so history has given you a wide, measured view," I supplied.

"Yes," she said, putting down her fork. "I suppose one could put it that way."

She stood and went over to the window, running her hand along the iron balcony. "You know," she said in a velvet voice, and in retrospect I guess that she felt obliged (because I had not asked) to present me with an anecdote about her mother, "there is a story they tell about my mother, and I never knew whether it was true. It seems that she was invited to a screening of a film, a documentary about her life. She was already quite frail then, and confined to a wheelchair. After the film was over, and as she was being helped into a car, a young woman flapped over to her to say, 'Oh, madame Colette, madame Colette, you've lived such a wonderful, wonderful life!' And my mother received the effusion, looked at her with those eyes, and was supposed to have answered, 'Really, it did not *seem* so while I was living it.'" Then she paused. "She couldn't have meant it, of course," she added.

Throughout the years we saw each other in Paris or Rome or Beaumont-du-Gâtinais, where she had rented a country house. I once ran into her in Marrakesh while she was staying at the Mamounia. Even there, she seemed to occupy the territory like a true colonial, insisting on feeding the gaunt stray cats who assembled around her lunch table at the pool. The management slitted its eyes with scorn, warning her that if she continued this she would be asked to leave the hotel. She exulted, I think, in risking it, and when I left, she was still feeding the cats.

It was while I was staying in Florida, along the Gulf of Mexico, that I saw from my beach-level window a figure walking along the sand with the purposefulness that singularized Colette. The sky was overcast, a strong tropical wind bent the palm trees, and a computerized pattern of whitecaps covered the dark mass of ocean. I rushed out to her, noticing immediately an unexpected change. Her face seemed blurred and the eyes looked anxious. Then I realized from something that she said, and even more by the things left unsaid, that she was seriously ill. Hoping to get some sun, she had stopped in Sarasota on her way back to Paris from a Houston hospital. We arranged to have dinner at her hotel.

"Hi!" said the waiter that evening. "My name is Craig. I'd like to recite tonight's specials."

I watched Colette carefully as he went through his performance. Her still-sharp gaze was fastened on him, and her faint smile collapsed into a heavy sigh in the silence that followed his prolonged exit. Toying first with her spoon and then with her wineglass, she shook her head in bewilderment, summing up her reaction in a single word: "America," she said wearily.

I said, "You always claimed that we exaggerate."

"It is difficult," she said in a weary voice. "These strange, spread-out cities, all shopping malls and no center, and everyone so unbelievably overweight and friendly. In Houston everyone called me by my first name! The city itself seemed as large as an entire country. Yes, I suppose I do think that you exaggerate. And now look at this . . ."

A first course, unrequested, was cheerfully brought to our table. "*Enjoy!*" advised the waiter, setting down a wide wedge of iceberg lettuce topped with beansprouts and bacon bits.

Colette grunted. *It Had to Be You* played on the piped-in music. She tried to smile.

"*Dépaysée,*" she said, out of my element, as though wryly defeated by it all, the vast spaces of America, the newness everywhere, and the sheer volume of it; the lantern-lit dining room with its free-and-easy waiters and its starter salad. And all at once her shape, form, size seemed to alter, wilting, so far from the piazzetta and the Palais-Royal, and I was moved by her sudden ill-humored vulnerability: she, finally now, the foreigner. Maybe this is what I had been in my dark times in Europe when my enthusiasms no longer served me and its mysteries had dimmed, and it was no fun to battle it any longer.

It was the last time I saw her, my European, for she died the following spring. We had never really made our peace, and I often miss our calling to each other across the wise, impenetrable sea that separated us even as we had faced each other at café tables and dining tables, across rooms and gardens; even as we had stood in cosmic isolation, face to face on the narrow back streets of Capri, almost touching.

Privileged
People

The first time I went to Paris was in the 1950s and I went there to sing. The singing job was offered to me by mail.

The letter, written in a penurious script, said, still says, "I hear you're a talented kid who sings and you want to come to Paris. They love Americans over here. A great voice isn't all that necessary and no one can make it in Paris on their voice alone. However, a personality is very important. The Mars Club is just off the Champs-Elysées on a dead end. The place is no joint. It's a small room with twenty-odd tables, dark and intimate, and we get a smart clientele. I don't know if you're acquainted with the prices of artistes over here. But I'll tell you right now, that if you're thinking of coming to Paris you're going to have to work for kicks and cakes. Entertainers don't make much but they're invited out a lot. I can offer you an engagement at 3,500 francs a night. That works out to be about $70 a week. Don't think it's stingy of me, because it isn't."

I remember smiling at the word *artistes*, and I certainly thought the offer was stingy. Also I was puzzled by the kicks and cakes, looking in such obscure comments (as I suppose I still do) for some sexual implication. I must have written back asking for more money, because the second

letter offers me a salary of $120. The club's owner, an
American named Jacobson, had learned about me through
a man who ran a New York supper club, Le Ruban Bleu.

Jacobson's letter continued: "Naturally I'll have to line
up the newspapers for your opening, so I'd appreciate your
answer as to the date of June 12. Yours very kindly.

"P.S. Please have a hundred of the enclosed cards made
up and hand them out on the boat coming over to Paris. If
you're coming to Paris, that is."

Paris. The word whirled wondrously in my head, the
sweeping *s* of its tail spinning it high above the flowering
chestnuts into the imagined sky of the Ile de France. How
full of radiance it seemed! But I am getting ahead of my
story.

The job in Paris seems to have come about so easily,
seamlessly. In those days, before I was twenty, did everything slide into place as easily as I remember? Certainly I
had my private worries. The most obsessive torment those
days was the possibility of being drafted into the Army.
Each day I would come home to savagely attack the letters
on the front-hall table. And finally the dreaded envelope
arrived. I was summoned, in that pre-Paris winter, to a gi-
gantic office above Madison Square Garden. Women
typed and listened without interest to young men who
slouched and pleaded without hope. I waited on a bench,
unable to keep my limbs still, until someone distractedly
pointed me to the rear of the room where yet another
draft-age kid was rising from his chair to stumble out of
the office. When I got there the girl at the desk did not
bother to look up.

"It says on your form that you have a complaint," she
began, "that you don't think you should be called into the
Army because you have, ah, headaches, and that you suffer

from nervous tension." Then she allowed herself to glance over at me. "What book did you look that up in?"

It was a chiseled face with lozenge eyes, a broad nose and a mouth commonly referred to as generous. She was then called a Negro and now called a black but actually she was brown.

"Headaches. Migraine h-headaches," I stuttered. "I get them and they make me unable to, ah, to . . ."

"To cope," she said. "They make you unable to cope. Sit down."

I obliged.

"Now," she began, with firm patience. "You've come into this office to tell me . . ."

"That I shouldn't go into the Army," I said, blurting it out right away. "I don't think it would do them any good or me any good. It panics me. I have claustrophobia about being cooped up. I know I should keep my mouth shut. I need to be left on my own. I don't know how else to say it. I just think it would be, ah, it would be . . ."

"A bad idea," she concluded. She narrowed her eyes. "Stand up," she said.

I stood.

"Now, sit down. Hmm. You seem to be able to sit and stand and obey orders."

I rubbed my forehead as though testing my skull. I still do not know how much of this performance was legitimate and how much was theater.

"Everyone gets headaches," she said, her smoky voice now without an edge. "I have a headache right now."

"I'm not surprised," I said. "It's this atmosphere here. Everyone's taking down information to s-send us all to places we don't want to be."

"That's enough of that. You don't have to s-stutter for me."

I clamped my jaw shut.

"And also, I have bursitis," she added, to fill in the silence. "In my elbow."

We looked at each other with sympathy. I thought she was the most seductive-looking girl I had ever seen.

"I don't know why I'm telling you all my troubles," she said. "I mean, about my elbow."

"It's probably from picking up those files," I said, allowing myself a smile. "Look. That's my file on your desk. You can send me off to a camp in Georgia with it, you can even send me to the Far East." Then I added, too self-confident by now. "I'd rather go to Paris."

"Keep your voice down," she said sharply. "For an eighteen-year-old you seem awfully sure of yourself."

"I'm covering up my . . ."

"Insecurities," we said at the same time. Then we stared at each other, sizing each other up.

"As it happens," she said, "*I* am the one who's going to Paris."

A groan of envy escaped me.

"I am going to Paris," she repeated, lowering her lids with satisfaction. "*Paris* has never seen anything like *me!*"

The remark would haunt me. "But what about me?" I said angrily. "You go to Paris and I go into the Army."

"You're a stranger to me," she said. "All of you are. That's how I manage to keep this job. That's how I saved enough money to go to Paris!" She opened a desk drawer and then slammed it shut for emphasis. Then, more quietly, she said, "Now what, exactly, would you have me do with your file?"

"Hide it," I answered without hesitating. "Hide it so it can never be found."

"You're saying that to *me*. To *me?* Here in the Draft Board?"

I nodded. My face was on fire.

"Do you mean?" she asked, fake-conspiratorial, "hide it away *foah-evah?*"

A military self wearing an impeccable uniform appeared in my mind, saluted, clicked its heels together, spun sharply around, and marched toward a very high wall. Then quickly, shedding guns and ammunition and khaki clothes, it leaped high in the air, up and over the wall, naked, unrestrained, and hotfooted it toward the sunset and whatever waited there.

I sighed. "But I guess you can't do that," I said, meaning it.

Then she began to laugh. It was a glorious thing to see and hear. She laughed with her whole body, a knee-slapping, laundry-flapping laugh. "Well, lookah you," she said between spasms. "A stranger comes in here and tells me that he'd rather go to Europe! Then he tells me to hide his file! *Who* do you think you *are?*" She was off again in peals of laughter. I laughed along with her, though I wasn't sure why.

No, we did not remain strangers. After the laughter she told me that her name was Olivia Lowell. It was about two weeks later that she agreed to go with me to the movies. That night she confided that her Tarot cards had been read the week I walked into her office, *warning* her about me. I was flattered. It was the first in a series of occult revelations she would make throughout the years.

I think I can still retrace the steps we took that winter when we met in the near-dark of the Astor Bar to hurry down the cold streets near Times Square. "I'd Walk A Mile," it said on the Camel sign above us, blowing a smoke ring two stories high. We searched for cheap restaurants where no one bothered us very much or gave us any of the black-white trouble of the time. When we were edged out of places, we tried shouting phrases about equality and America and who did they think they were, but we always lost those arguments and had to leave.

Elliot Kaplan, a friend of mine, gave me the key to a seldom-used run-down apartment in Chelsea. The place was not his, and he used it for his secret life away from home. Olivia and I received Elliot's key with gratitude, trying to forget about what our families would say, for each of us still lived at home. Here we were alone, eating and drinking and swallowing each other up as the winds wailed through that roach-ridden place until the big-faced alarm clock shrilled its message from the rickety bureau. Then we reassembled into our neatly pressed selves, rushing to the subway so that Olivia could be home by midnight, surely one of the more exotic Cinderellas on the BMT.

In March, as planned, Olivia left for Europe. Two months later I was offered the singing job in Paris. I know that along the way something happened to my file—maybe it was karmic and maybe it wasn't, but we never talked about it again. One day I received a form letter advising me that I was definitively ineligible for the armed forces.

It was my first morning in Paris. Only one eye was properly open and it had opened slowly. The other was shielded by my arm, for I have always slept that way, as though warding off a bad spirit. I had opened my eye slowly on purpose, letting the lashes graze against the unyielding roll at the head of the bed. I had not understood why there was no pillow on the bed when I went to sleep the night before, arriving on the boat train. It must have been one of their eccentricities, I thought. The French! The French! They do not sleep with pillows! I mumbled this deliriously into the air.

I knew, and had known throughout my dreams that first night in Paris, that the window would be just across from the bed, and I wanted to approach the view slowly, giving it as much time as possible because it would be my first view in daylight. So I lay still on the bed trying to postpone Paris now that it was really there, allowing myself to hear it, to inhale the room. Was it furniture wax that had given it such a puzzling, provocative odor?

I turned to the wall, both eyes now open. There were two wallpapers. Pale shepherdesses and faded farms competed with prickly paisleys, bright as flags. An immense mirrored armoire, prudently chained against the slanted floor, leaned murderously toward the foot of the bed. I looked at it; it looked back at me. In an instant I was up, next to the window, looking out at the rooftops.

Orange awnings sprouted against the grey buildings and everywhere there were geraniums. I could not see the street. But the leaden sky was overpowering. There was too much of it; it was too unmanageable, too full of history. I saw a tricolor somewhere in the jumble of rooftops as I heard a knock on my door. Then, without waiting, indifferent to my possible *entrez* or *attendez*, a woman arrived bearing coffee and a croissant on a battered tray. She glanced at me standing naked in front of the window, said, "*Voilà!*" as she set down the tray on the bureau, hesitated before retreating, and added, in a melody of the topmost notes in her register, "*Mais vous êtes beau! Que vous êtes beau et mince! Et quel zizi!*" Thus singing, she withdrew.

I had not flinched. I looked down to see that all this time I had been aroused. I was in Paris. I was nineteen. Throbbing, I took my coffee cup of cobalt blue and sat on the edge of the bed. The croissant flaked all over the sheets as I bit into it. The bedcover, my thighs, were covered with what fell. The biting coffee burned my lips. My lips were on fire and I was clothed only in pastry crumbs and Paris waited outside my window. I removed each single crumb, licking my fingers before they returned to my sheet, to my body. I groaned with so much pleasure that I wondered at the corner of my mind whether it would kill me.

Olivia had not met me when I got off the ship, as we had planned. Instead, she called my hotel from Munich, saying darkly that she was *in trouble* but not to *worry*, that she'd *explain* and would arrive in plenty of time for my opening night. She then hung up. Her voice sounded more dramatic than I'd remembered, but I thought that it might have been the novelty of talking from one European country to another. I was pleased that she hadn't been in Paris for those first days because I wanted to discover it on my own.

The owner of the Mars Club, Jake Jacobson, was an American who had fought in France during the Second World War and stayed behind in Paris, marrying a woman who, it was rumored, had been a collaborationist. After the liberation (they said) her head had been shaved. The only reason anyone found for Jacobson's having married the woman was that she was French, and this allowed him to open a nightclub in Paris. She sulked nightly behind the register. Her hair was cropped short, she wore tight black dresses, and she rubbed the back of her neck with ringed fingers. Barefoot because her feet hurt, she kept her shoes under the ledgers. She was an odd counterpart to big Jacobson, a fleshy man whose large head joined his body with no visible connecting link. He sweated all the time and kept mopping his brow and his heavy cheeks with no remedial effect. He talked loud and fast and sometimes humorously, and he was crazy about jazz music, singers, nightlife, and so on. When I walked into the Mars Club that first afternoon, my sheet music under my arm, his first three questions were whether I'd had the cards printed up, how many of them I had given out on the boat, and how much I'd paid.

The club, like most nightclubs in Paris, was a cave bats might have flown to. No light entered it, even at high noon when its small door opened to admit liquor crates and the cleaning woman. It was crowded opening night and I'm sure I was very nervous, but I cannot remember much of it beyond worrying that the waiter I tipped would follow me with the spotlight, from the barstool, where I began to sing, up the two steps next to the pianist, where the rest of the songs took place. I launched my palm to the audience on the first *you,* in *You Go to My Head,* and left it there, waiting for *the bubbles in a glass of champagne* to retrieve it. My staging, unsurveilled, was rudimentary. One of the Paris critics wrote that when I sang I sounded like a child of many divorces.

In the split second before the applause for the last song, I heard a sultry, familiar voice say loudly, "Fan*tas*tic. *He is* fan*tas*tic!," effectively managing to take the attention away from me to plant it directly on herself. It was Olivia.

The change was astonishing. She was seated at a dark

table with two smarmy gentlemen, indistinguishable from each other. I remember very clearly that she was wearing a dress of white crepe that fit her, I said, hoping to shock her escorts, like a contraceptive. Her hair, usually carefully, painfully straightened, had been cut to within an inch of her skull, so that the shape of her head was like a serpent's. Were it not for the shock, were it not for such a blatant defiance of the conventional (and it seems I was prepared at the time to be a renegade but not a radical), I would have found her ravishingly beautiful.

"Well, well," I said, sliding into an empty chair.

"Is that all you can say? I mean, *I'm* prepared to say that *you* were *won*derful, that you've *nev*ah looked better. *Nev*ah!"

"Thanks," I said. "Excuse me, Olivia. Excuse me. You've, ah, changed. You look so . . ."

"Different," she said. I had forgotten how she finished my sentences. "More theatrical, is what you mean."

I nodded.

"You mean, I used to be a nice quiet colored girl. Just a nice quiet colored girl in New York. But here!" She drew circles in the air with her long fingers. "Here in Europe, I mean, I've become an exotic creature everyone wants to know. And touch! In Switzerland they came over to *touch* me, to see whether the color would come off! I've been asked to appear in a film. And to model. You see. You *see*. *You're* not the only one. Everything is different now. You can't possibly know what it's like, the change. You can't possibly know."

I said I guess not. I had also forgotten that Olivia repeated almost every word she emphasized.

She never got around to introducing me to the two men at the table. She had become too self-absorbed to bother with such formalities. Later, toward dawn, Olivia sat in bed smoking. I had moved to an inexpensive pension on the rue Marignan not far from the club.

"You remember when I called you from Munich? Well, I was being followed by a man. A man who I had said *excuse me* to, in a hotel lobby. Just *excuse me*, because he was standing in my way. He fell in love with me *then and there*. He followed me around Munich in one of those little humpbacked cars they have there, carrying a small leather valise. And you know what was in the valise? Guess! *Money!* A suitcase filled with money. And you know why? He robbed a bank. He robbed a bank so he'd have enough money to take care of me, once we actually met. Of *me!* Olivia Lowell!" She inhaled a blast of smoke from her cigarette.

"But you've probably wondered how we finally *met*. Well . . ." She paused for effect, stubbing out her cigarette and placing the saucer on the lamp table next to the bed. "He finally got up the courage and sat next to me at a café along the—get this pronunciation—Thea*ti*nerstrasse. He sat next to me and told me that he had stolen this money for *me*. He told me this after we discussed the weather and the quality of the coffee. I mean, he just blurted it out! I said, of course, that he was crazy. I laughed politely. But then he opened his valise *and it was filled with money!* Piles of money in neat little rows. I've never seen so much money except in a bank . . ."

"Which is where it came from," we said at the same time.

"Well!" she continued. "It's very hard, when someone has taken all that trouble, not to sit and have a coffee at his table. Don't you agree? Are you listening to what I am saying? Well, they came and arrested him the next day at the same café. I saw them do it. I told him I might come back the next day to the same place at the same time, and I did. I was so curious, you see. I mean, it was so *foreign*, the idea. So just when I was about to sit down next to him—he was already smiling, pulling out a chair for me—the police came along! Two of them. One on each side."

She sighed, putting her hand on her forehead and her head further into the pillow. "I stood there dumbfounded. They just took him into a car, along with his valise. He never looked back. And you know what I did? Broke as I was, I paid the little bill on his table, drank the rest of his coffee, and left. But think of the poor man! There he is, languishing in a jail in Munich, all because he fell in love with a colored girl from America."

Then Olivia burst out laughing. "If you could have seen his face when he opened the valise. He was so *proud* of himself! I was so—how can I say it. So *touched!*"

She searched in the saucer for the smoldering cigarette, stubbed it out again, snuggled against me with wonderful self-satisfaction, and just before falling asleep asked me, for the dozenth time, what I thought of her new haircut, inspired, she repeated, by an African girl she had passed on the street in Montparnasse.

I have often wondered whether Olivia was, as she sometimes claimed, the first American girl—the first *evolved* American girl—to wear an Afro. She certainly got a lot of mileage out of it that summer, and if she considered it revolutionary, perhaps it was, even though the effect was more cosmetic than political. Revolutions, reforms, alterations in society often spring forth from such humble things as vanity. It is true that she was spectacular. It is also true that the son of the Sultan of Marrakesh asked her to marry him after seeing her in the lobby of the Claridge Hotel on the Champs-Elysées. She might have been tempted, but she quickly learned that he had eight other wives, and the plan fell through, just as the man in Munich and his valiseful of money fell through, and I realized very quickly that though Olivia was, as they say, wined and dined, she seemed to return almost every night to the solidity of the simple pension I chose to call home that summer.

The pension was so aggressively modest that it had no name. On the street level the row of buttons simply listed *Pension, quatrième étage*. Its owners were a joyless middle-aged couple named Koffman, too old in spirit to cope with Philippe, a young son of sixteen. Koffman was an Austrian Jew, an intellectual with courtly manners who read most of the day in a large, comfortable chair, with antimacassars on the armrests and *Der Rosenkavalier* on the victrola. He had fled Vienna in the late thirties, arriving in Paris to find work driving a taxi. His wife, a Parisian, had transformed an inherited sprawling apartment into an unsuccessful pension. She was a plump, kind woman, unusual in Parisians, where kindness was famously rare. She walked slowly and tired easily, and when she went out to do the day's shopping she would try to persuade Philippe to go along with her to carry the packages. The Koffmans must have existed on very little money, since we were the only guests at their nameless pension.

Koffman's chair was placed carefully next to the one uncurtained window in the sitting room and he waved pleasantly without looking up from his historical volumes whenever Olivia or I passed the door. The place reminded me of the meandering, lightless apartments on New York's West Side, where exiled Middle Europeans moved restlessly from one room to another remembering what once had been. Staying at the pension, I now saw that they had achieved the same disconsolate atmosphere they had correctly believed they had left behind.

"*You Americans!*" Koffman began unexpectedly one day from out of the shadows of the sitting room. "You're so full of life! You come over here with no idea of how weary this place is, how often it has been ruined and put back together again, and then blown apart."

"Not Paris," put in the wife as she came down the dark corridor. "Paris has always been spared."

Koffman said, "You know how many died in the First World War, how many French?"

I said that I did not know, impatiently shifting my weight from one foot to the other as I stood in the doorway craving the sunlit streets. I did not want to think about the dead.

"One out of twenty-five people! One out of twenty-five!"

"Like a plague," said Mme. Koffman, bending under my arm to enter the sitting room. "In every city in France there is a monument to the dead. In every village as well. France is like a cemetery."

"Hah," croaked Koffman. "This young man wishes to be out among the young people and not talk of death with us. You are what is known as a night person. Yes?"

"I guess so," I said. "I work at night, if that's what you mean."

"Then you ought to be happy staying at our pension. We keep this place dark, eh?" He held a book in his hand, his index finger crooked into the page. Mended eyeglasses were perched on the edge of his thinning hair.

I nodded.

"I spent the last two years of the war hiding in this dark apartment. But I'm sure you don't wish to hear about that either. In America you always have bright lights, I've been given to understand. You don't worry as much as we do about consequences, you Americans." Then he added in an undertone, "Like our son Philippe. He never thinks about tomorrow. He lives only day to day. He rushes about without care. He never considers where he has come from or where he is going, but only the steps he takes. Am I wrong to make this *analogie* to America?"

I did not know the answer, I said, hoping to end the encounter. "We live in the present, if that's what you mean."

The conversation remained suspended there, in that dimly lit room: Koffman in his worn, upholstered chair, and myself, the young American standing in the doorway, too polite to leave, longing to be in the brilliant Paris of Hemingway's back table at the Deux Magots, the Paris of painters in garrets and long sunlit hours at those same sidewalk cafés discussing shadowy things like existentialism, which we did not, could not, do not still quite understand. We had all come to Europe for that, and it was too late.

"The past," I muttered to Koffman, unsure of myself, "is why we come here."

"*Ja, ja.*" He nodded, moving his head, it seemed, with effort.

And once there, once finally in Europe, we rushed around like birds let loose in a temple, not knowing where to perch, what was sacred, profane. We remained mostly up in the rafters. But we did not care to listen to Koffman's weary views.

I said, "I've got to leave."

"Of course," Koffman replied, releasing me with a smile.

I escaped from the darkness of those rooms into the streets of Paris below.

Koffman's patched and mended vision of Europe particularly upset Olivia. She began to fuss over his son Philippe, telling him lengthy imaginative tales about America to compensate, she thought, for the gloomy atmosphere of his home. These stories were told in a mixture of some half-remembered Creole French and English. I always suspected that Philippe's English was fine, and that his game was to pretend not to understand Olivia so that these conversations might be prolonged. One Sunday, we invited him to a picnic.

But I have not described Philippe. He was, at sixteen, tall for his age, almost my height, and very pale. No wonder, considering his confinement. On his mischief-making unfinished child's face, his sharp eyes shone like a fox's. When he turned his head and the clever glint was obscured, he had the most vulnerable neck imaginable.

The sky was grey that Sunday as we set off toward the Bois de Boulogne in the borrowed Deux Chevaux.

I said, "It's getting cloudy."

"Don't say it's going to rain," said Olivia. "I know that's what you're going to say. *Now*"—she turned to the back seat—"listen to *me*, Philippe. This is going to be *fun*."

"Olivia," I pleaded.

"Now say it after me," she continued, still turning toward the back seat. "This is going to be *fun . . .*"

It was when we were outside Paris, driving through the countryside on a small road, that a chicken surprised us by running halfway across the road.

"Why does the chicken cross the road?" asked Olivia as I jammed my foot on the weak brake. "That's what we say in America," she announced, "though I don't know why."

The chicken stayed in the middle of the road watching the car. The three of us stared at the chicken.

"It doesn't budge," said Philippe.

"We can't sit here all day gaping at a chicken," said Olivia.

It seemed clear that the chicken was waiting for us to pass. And just as my foot hit the accelerator and we began to move, the chicken crossed in front of the car and was crushed under the left front wheel. As I drove away there was a terrible silence inside the car. The three of us turned around to see the mound of feathers gradually receding in the distance.

"It couldn't be avoided," I said.

"*Destiny!*" said Olivia in her darkest voodoo voice. "I can *feel* it. The same thing is going to happen to us, to you and me. No matter what we might think, you're going to drive off into the sunset and I'm going to be lying at the side of the road."

We found a field bright with poppies. An overgrown driveway led to a large abandoned stucco house whose design bore some distant resemblance to the château at Fontainebleau not far away. We spread out our picnic things on the grass and lay on our backs.

"He's beautiful," said Olivia, tilting her head in the direction of Philippe.

"He has beautiful manners," I said. "All these kids in Paris seem to have beautiful manners."

"I don't mean manners," said Olivia. "Why don't you admit that he's beautiful. You're too vain. That's it."

"Okay, he's beautiful," I said.

"He pays attention to me and listens to what I say, which is more than I can say for you."

I leaned over and opened the jar of salade Niçoise that Mme. Koffman had prepared that morning.

"Because you're out there flirting with all of Paris," she continued. "Would you pass me the bread, please?"

Olivia broke off a piece of bread and very carefully covered it with pâté. "*Une baguette,*" she said to Philippe. "*N'est-ce pas?*" Butter, appropriately, would have melted in her mouth.

"*Une baguette,*" he echoed, smiling back.

"When I talk to him, he's *mine,* then. Do you understand?" insisted Olivia. "You're not mine. You're too busy being everybody's."

"You're a fine one to talk," I shouted. "I'll give you about a minute to keep quiet. Meanwhile, quit trying to start an argument and put some salad on the plates. It's going to rain."

In France, as the Impressionists knew, the meadows and fields shimmer, the poppies blur with color, there is a diffusion in the air that does not exist farther north, where landscapes are clearly defined, carefully etched against the sky. That summer day fragments in my memory into filtered images of the three of us sitting on a blanket, then walking into the humming fields, a haze screening the poplars edging the property. The house had been left to deteriorate and looked as though it had been abandoned during the war. AMERICANS GO HOME was written on one of the outside walls.

> "*Je l'aime*
> *Je l'aime un peu*
> *Je l'aime à la folie*
> *Je l'aime pas du tout*
> *Je l'aime . . .*"

Philippe held out a daisy, meticulously pulling away a petal at a time.

"In America," said Olivia, passing a hand across the cropped hair on her head, "we just say 'he loves me, he loves me not.' You can see the difference in our culture *right there*."

Philippe did not listen. His devilish child's face was bent toward the flower with concentration as he repeated his phrases, the down on his neck pale gold in the sunlight. When he was displeased with the answer he picked up another flower. "*Voilà!*" he shouted. "*Je l'aime à la folie! Je l'aime à la folie!*"

He suddenly leapt up and began to run, taking off across the fields in front of the house with amazing speed, his tall blond figure cutting into the high grasses.

"Wait!" I called.

"No!" said Olivia quickly. "Let him run for a while. He's always cooped up in that depressing pension with those dismal parents and he hardly ever has the chance to go free."

I looked after him with envy. "Every now and then you're right," I said.

We walked back to our picnic blanket and lay back on the grass and saw in the distance a large storm cloud quickly covering the sky.

"You're right too," said Olivia. "Some of the time. It *is* going to rain."

A sudden wind sprang up, rushing across the fields like an invisible herd, bending the sea of grasses as it advanced. The leaves on the trees in front of the house pulled at their branches and the sky darkened and then grew black.

I called to Philippe but the wind pulled my voice back, carrying it along with the dust and leaves that blew in our faces. Our napkins and paper cups went scattering along the path leading to the house.

"Leave them, leave them. We'll pick it all up later,"
shouted Olivia. "Philippe! *Come back this minute!*" she
commanded to the rushing winds. Then the rain came at
once. I began to run across the fields, trying to follow
Philippe's path.

"It's all right," said Olivia, running up behind me. "It's
just a cloudburst. He'll hide someplace until it's over, just
as we will. Come on, come on into the house. We're getting soaked. I can hardly see with the rain in my eyes.
Stop worrying. There's nothing we can do about it right
now anyway."

But we each turned to call out to Philippe once more as
we ran up the path.

And so we went into the unlocked house, and once inside we climbed the wide staircase past the big empty
rooms, and we found a small bedroom with a shred of
worn, mildewed carpet on the floor, and, finding that, we
lay down on it, close to each other. It seemed inevitable
that the room in the corner of the abandoned house had
been waiting for us. The sound of the rain, and the
unearthly darkness, and the dampness of our bodies con-
spired to make us forget everything else, blocking from
our minds the grownup concerns about open car windows,
the now inedible picnic things on the soaking blanket, and
Philippe. I studied the glint of moisture on the edge of
Olivia's lips, feeling myself drawn again into that
smoothest of chasms, spinning around dream-like as the
rain pounded against the broken window; we found ourselves in some primeval place where we punished each
other and were forgiven, punished each other and were
forgiven. We wanted, I think, to use each other up, for we
knew that what we had begun in America was now
doomed and would not last the summer.

"I want to die," said Olivia. "I want to die right here during this storm in this unknown house, with that boy lost forever in the fields, leaving it all unfinished. When we first knew each other our one thought was to come to Europe. Everything was Europe. We never thought beyond it. I want you to die here with me so that nothing can ever be better for you than this."

I turned over and looked at the ceiling, concentrating on a small branch that had worked its way inside through a broken pane.

"I don't want to die now," I said. "Not just yet."

She brought me back to her, our hearts flapping their wings together. "Don't you see that this is the best moment, while everything, *everything* is ahead of us? And we would never have to see any of it destroyed," she whispered. In one graceful motion she stood. I lay on the floor looking up at her, a priestess of the wilderness towering above me. I held her calves, my head against her feet, terrified in that instant of being alone.

"It's stopped raining," she said in a calm voice, looking down at me. In the pale light from the window I saw the look of triumph on her face, reveling in my sudden need.

Proud, too proud, I quickly stood, all affection gone from my face, from my body. "And we have to look for the kid," I said, exhaling with exasperation, sweeping the hair out of my eyes and struggling quickly into my clothes.

We looked. We crossed and recrossed the fields. We went around to the back of the house, where we passed an ancient black Citroën with weeds growing through its windows and doors. We searched through the ruined gardens and we trampled into the woods beyond. Then we

walked slowly to the house and sat on the small brick staircase next to the back door.

"He's lost," said Olivia. "We brought him here and we
lost him. We brought him here because we wanted him to
love us. We want everyone to love us all the time, children
and animals included. We can never get enough, either of
us."

I shrugged. Maybe she was right.

"*What are we doing in Europe anyway?* What am *I*
doing here? I want to go back to America and just be a
nigger."

"Olivia," I began, trying to be reasonable. "You're not
making any sense."

"How do you know?" she shouted. "How do you know
what an effort it is to go around like a freak so I can watch
people pay attention to me, *notice* me . . ."

"Why is it any different for you? All of us who've
come here want to be noticed. We pretend that we came
here for the culture but we end up showing off. That's
what they expect from us anyway . . ."

"I want to go home," she interrupted. "I want to be a
colored girl who marries a colored man and has colored
children in a colored neighborhood!" She was screaming
by now.

"Then why did you bother coming here? Why did you
bother coming to Europe?" I shouted back.

But I never knew her answer. All the shouting awak-
ened Philippe, who had fallen asleep in the derelict car
parked in the overgrown driveway. He opened the car
door and it creaked on its hinges. Then he unfolded his
long form and came toward us.

"Did you think I was lost?" he asked with a grin.

"We did," said Olivia angrily. "It was very mean of you

not to come back when it started to rain. We are responsible for you, after all. Now we've been fighting."

He looked us up and down. "Here, I picked some flowers. You can each have half."

Olivia ran her long fingers through his hair. "You don't know which of us you like better, do you?" she said in a kind voice. "Take *him*." She motioned in my direction. "He's white. He's terrific."

"Thank you," I said with mock formality, bowing.

We went around to the front of the house to the meadow where the blanket was and picked up some paper cups. Then we stood on the wet grass looking at the sky, waiting to see whether the sun would come out again. But the grey remained. I poured us each some wine.

"Well, here's looking at you, kid," I said, toasting Olivia, toasting Philippe.

"That's something we say in America," Olivia began.

I rolled my eyes over at her.

"Humphrey Bogart says it in *Casablanca*. I could have *moved* to Casablanca this week to marry a sultan's son, but I chose not to. What do you think of *that?* Now, try repeating it. 'Here's looking at you, kid.'"

Eventually Philippe mastered the phrase and we heard it all the way home in the car.

The haze returned the next day, and the next, and soon Paris was under a yellowish pall. It was during this miasma cloaking the city, cloaking my spirits as well, that I would take buses, jumping onto the open platforms just to keep in motion. Once she had seen the Winged Victory and the Mona Lisa, Olivia stayed away from museums and churches, preferring public places, mainly cafés, where she and I would sit in prominent positions. We quarreled, sometimes discreetly.

Late at night we went for pleasant drives in a borrowed convertible, the faint night breezes fluttering the scarves Olivia then wore. They became a ritual, those late-night journeys, the quiet streets unraveling like black ribbons pinned into place by phosphorescent squares and circles. Usually we headed toward the quarter I most cherished, Les Halles, past the arcades of the rue du Louvre, the sleeping *clochards,* Zola's "gently sighing *pissotières,* pale lighthouses of damp and foggy nights," and into the heart of Paris, its marketplace, where radishes were displayed like rubies.

I did not analyze my restlessness those long, humid days. During the afternoons the sky went from yellow to ocher. Throughout Paris, trees were uprooted, the streets broadened for the cars. The systematic pruning of chestnuts had begun, and their freshly stunted branches clawed at the stale air just above the boulevards. I walked along the river and looked at the boats. A few men fished in the languid current; small houseboats and barges moved slowly past, and above the embankment cars clogged the Place de la Concorde. Ahead of me the twin towers of Notre-Dame were menacing, reaching up from their island, above the rooftops, a giant bat waiting for the darkness to make its flight. A small crowd had gathered along the quay a short distance away. Their collective stance, a frozen huddling, suggested fear, as though a monumental wave was about to rise from the Seine to carry them away. Above us, threading through the sound of traffic, was an intermittent high-low howl from a police car or an ambulance. I looked from the crowd on the quay to the river.

I have retained a clear memory of that image, inseparable from its accompaniment, the siren on the square above, now growing louder, as, with a shrill cry, an ambulance stopped on the sidewalk. Almost within arm's reach floated the drowned body of a young man. His hand was cupped under his chin, as though deep in thought. The hand rose and fell with the slow current, each time bathing the face with water.

Backing away as the stretcher bearers came quickly down the steps, I then turned, rushing up to the boulevard, where I ducked into the Métro in an insane dash to get back to the darkness and safety of the pension.

When I got to the fourth floor I walked quickly down the corridor to my room. I had been told earlier in the day that the Koffmans were going to be away until late that evening. Olivia, I knew, had gone to a film studio to see about a job. I desperately wanted to be alone and yet I was overwhelmed by loneliness. A hum of silence filled the hallways and the heavily curtained sitting room. When I got to my door I hesitated, the key in my hand. The palest of light outlined the doorframe, and my door, usually locked, was not quite closed.

A sound came from inside, a muffled, rhythmic sound, and I heard my name and then Olivia's name murmured. I knew, as I pushed open the door, that the voice was Philippe's. His clothes were around his ankles and his head was buried in our pillows. Underneath his arched, lean body his hand moved swiftly. Quickly I tried to close myself out of the room, to return to the darkness of the corridor. But his head jerked toward me as I stepped backward.

"You've come back," he said, startled. "I thought you were out all day. Both of you. I was *sure* you said you'd be out all day . . ."

"Listen, Philippe," I said. "You ought to be in your own room, you know. I mean, it's all right. But you ought . . ." I could not finish what I was saying.

"I came in here to read. I like being in your room. Then I don't know. I just started, well . . ."

"It's okay, Philippe." I was very tense. There were no lights on in the room and the yellowish pall of the afternoon seemed to have settled on the furniture, on the bed.

"I wanted to make believe," he said. His fox's eyes stayed on me. "I wanted to make believe I was both of you. I guess you know what I mean."

"I guess I know what you mean," I said, my voice unsteady.

I sat down on the bed next to him. Now the place felt suffocatingly warm. The curtains clotted the windows, the hallway was haunted by darkness; cooking odors had been trapped for decades in the heavy unchangeable walls, in the thin carpets, in the sleazy bedspreads. Outside the window, barred by shutters, sprawled Paris, mired in its fusty, uncompromising past.

Philippe fell back on the bed, his face growing feverishly pink. I leaned over to look at him. "You've been here before with Olivia, haven't you?" I said, suddenly realizing how close to home our worldly betrayals had become. "Just the two of you . . . ?"

He nodded. "Just once. I begged her to teach me. . . . You Americans are so free," he said, lifting his hand to me and letting it fall.

"Stop saying *you Americans!*" I shouted. Then I allowed myself to look at him. "And now you want another kind of lesson."

His teeth were chattering. "There's no one here," he said. "You're both . . . Can I be Olivia for you?"

"No," I said quickly. Then slowly I watched my hand move across the smoothness of his shoulders, astonished to think that he was only three years younger than I.

"Even children and animals," I mumbled, remembering what Olivia had said that day of the picnic.

My hand traced across his chest and up the nape of his neck, closing around it. He blinked his eyes.

"I don't want you to be Olivia for me," I said, unable to control the huskiness in my voice. I held him hard, one hand on his neck and the other on his shoulder. Then I relaxed my grip and moved closer to him. "Just be Philippe. Do you understand?"

We stayed in the room until it was dark and we could no longer see each other.

That night I went to the Mars Club early, saw that only Jacobson was there, going over the books, and started to leave.

"Stay a minute," he said. "You're always in a rush to get out of here. I've never figured out where you're going."

"Neither have I," I admitted, reluctantly pulling up a chair.

"You know, sonny," he began (I think he called me sonny because he could never remember my name), "you're not doing as well as some of the other entertainers who've worked here."

"Uh-huh."

He looked at me carefully. "You look like a kid with a lot of luck," he said. "I thought it as soon as you walked in here. But you don't know how to use it."

I gave him a crooked smile.

"You could have anything you want in this town," he continued, drumming his heavy fingers on the small table.

"Anything at all. But you'll never get any of it because you don't really know what you want. And furthermore," he added as I was about to interrupt, "you don't know how to use what you've already got."

"What's got into you?" I said angrily. "I've been working here over a month and you haven't said more than a few words to me each night. Now all of a sudden you're psychoanalyzing me."

"I've been watching you," he said. "I may not seem to notice anything. But I do."

"That makes me feel fine. Just fine."

"Okay, I'm going to give it to you straight," he began. I winced. It was a line of dialogue I had only heard in the movies.

"You're a beautiful kid," he said. "Now, just shut up and listen to me. You know it. *I* know it. Everyone who comes in here knows it. I also know that it doesn't last. So it's time you talked about it and about what you're going to do about it. Most people who've got what you've got, in that combination, kill themselves before they're twenty-four. You know what I mean?"

I kept quiet. The memory of the boy floating in the Seine had kept me, would keep me awake at night.

"Or twenty-three," he added, after a moment of reflection. He took out a large patterned handkerchief and blew his nose.

"I'm glad I've still got some time left."

"Don't be such a smartass."

There was a long, uncomfortable silence. *Beauty* is a tricky word. I knew that when someone tells a woman she is beautiful, everything is fine and everyone is happy, except, perhaps, an unbeautiful woman nearby who overhears it and knows it is not meant for her. When a man is called beautiful it makes everyone angry, men and women alike. Even children hearing it think that someone has made a mistake with the language. Bad things are implied: narcissism, frivolousness, addled brains, suspicious sexuality. These were the payments that must be extracted to compensate for it. Beautiful men ought to be kept at home under wraps, like mad people, so that no one had to be disturbed by them. I knew all this one way since I was about eight, and another way since I was fifteen.

"I'm not," I said.

"Bullshit!" said Jake Jacobson. Then he sighed with impatience. "You're not going to make it as a singer because you're not interested enough. You're just playing with it. Most singers, and actors and models and all the other clowns in this business, are just classy hookers. You don't even care enough to bother. You get up there to sing as though you're singing to yourself."

"Look, Jake," I began, standing, "I don't need . . ."

"Yes, you do," he commanded. "Sit down. I'm not through. Come on, come on. Don't think you're so great that you can't stand criticism."

I sat down slowly.

"So half the people come in here to hear you sing, and half the people come in here to look at you. I need singers who get one hundred percent listeners. I'm running a music joint, not a horse show.

"I'm not knocking your singing," he said after a while. "You sing good."

There was another pause. "Why did you come to Europe? I mean, I know everyone wants to come to Paris, but why did you come?"

"I came to Europe to see Europe," I said lamely.

"Then see it. Get out of Paris and see it. I'm not firing

you. You can stay as long as you like. I'm suggesting." He mopped his brow with the big handkerchief. "I look after my entertainers," he said with feeling.

He then heaved himself out of his chair, dismissing me by going into the tiny kitchen just off the bar where he was known to prepare himself immense private meals of wursts and kraut and potatoes on a two-burner stove. "And take care of yourself out there on the streets, sonny," he called.

He was whistling *Lullaby of Birdland* when I walked out of the door.

Within the next two weeks everything seemed to fly apart at once. We moved out of the pension because Olivia felt that the place itself was responsible for some of our troubles; she was receiving hostile messages from its walls, she said. We found a hotel near the Etoile, never returning to see the Koffmans or Philippe again. Such was the measure of our carelessness.

Our new room was on the rue Chambiges. It was cramped, it gave onto a back court, and it was clear that we would get into further fights there. My guess is that we each longed for the final fight that would separate us. Olivia spent a great deal of time complaining about her wardrobe, the food—talking all the time about stomach cramps. Our last, bad afternoon happened when I came back to the room and found her sitting in her cat posture against the headboard of the bed. Surrounding her were neat piles of clothing and cosmetics. On the chair was an open suitcase.

"Where do you think you're going?" I asked in what I thought was a reasonable voice.

"Where do I *think* I'm going?" she asked, lazily reaching for a cigarette and lighting it. "Or where"—and here she blew an ominous cloud of smoke in my direction—"*am* I going." Her hands were shaking.

"Have it either way."

She sprang forward on her knees. "I've *had* it either way and I'm sick of it. I get the impression that you want to travel, and you've never even suggested that I go along with you. You're so self-centered . . ."

I started toward her.

"In the meanwhile, I, *me*, I've been asked on a trip. His/name/is/Raf." She was enunciating each word very sharply. "He/is/fantastic."

I moved my mouth but said nothing.

"I've been offered a modeling job in Milan. We will go first to Switzerland. He has a motorcycle big enough for two."

"Nice."

"It's red. *Red*. And he can go one hundred and forty kilometers an hour with it."

"You'll get yourself killed."

"Hah!"

I said, "You can do whatever you want. But you're not going anywhere on a motorcycle."

"No one tells me what to do. I'm not that little black sheep you picked up in New York."

Without hesitating I grabbed up the clothes and makeup that were on the bed, and in one motion dropped them into the open suitcase, took the suitcase to the window, and emptied it into the air.

She screamed, "I/AM/MY/WARDROBE! I/AM/ MY / MAKEUP! / YOU'VE / THROWN / ME / OUT/OF/THE/WINDOW!"

The next day we said a tearful goodbye, promising to meet sometime in Paris in the autumn. Then I went to the

Mars Club and quit my job. When I went back to the
hotel room I stood for a long while looking at the left-over
debris, wondering, of course, what we might have done,
should have done, could have done, did not do, would not
do, had postponed doing. Then I pushed the half-empty
cosmetic tubes and bottles aside and carefully unfolded a
map of Europe on the bed.

The trip I took, the places, the wonders blur into postcard images and snapshots, and even now I can only try to
imagine the brief scenes played out against various
significant backdrops. I have the photographs still. Whose
melting shadow (holding a camera) strides across the
tabletop, as I tilt back in my chair on the Piazza San
Marco? And in another picture, against the walls of Avila,
I pose with two lean figures who must have been all-im-
portant then and unremembered now. The walls rise above
us in the sunlight. The girl wears a wide-brimmed hat and
she is facing away from me; the boy is suntanned, blurred,
pointing to a place beyond the limits of the picture, and I
am following his indication to see . . . what?
    I took a train back to Paris in the early autumn, finding
myself a hotel room on the Quai Voltaire, a room just
under the roof, its windows looking out at a grey, in-
tensely blank wall. I roamed around Paris alone for a few
weeks. In the evenings I took with me a celestial chart
constructed out of cardboard, trying to figure out the constellations in the autumn sky.
    Paris had occupied such a vast place in my dreams the
previous year that now, alone, I understood that I was
finally there, stalking through it, staying up until dawn,
sleeping fitfully until the next expedition through its
streets, haunted by those same dreams still. I wanted to

leave it and return home to the world I knew, and I wanted desperately to stay there the rest of my life (the permanent world-weary adolescent sitting on a bench in the Place des Vosges, reading, methodically slitting open the pages of the books with a penknife as the wan sun burnished the chestnut trees and the world around me was comfortably ageing). After all, maybe this is what I had come to Paris for in the first place, this time alone with my head turned away from everyone. But eventually I made my plans to leave. Poverty is a frequent rescuer of the immobilized.

Through Jacobson, I discovered where Olivia was living and I telephoned her. The phone was answered by a Frenchman with an elegant Parisian accent. He was too cordial. When Olivia got on the line she sounded happy to hear from me, and we arranged to meet in the Jardin des Tuileries at the miniature boat basin. The afternoon was crisp and very beautiful. Late as always, Olivia came toward me without apologies.

"It isn't easy," she said. "You live nearer than I do. I'm in Trocadéro, near the Eiffel Tower. It *looms* up over the terrace. Oh, this is perfect. Fake little boats going around in circles, going nowhere. No, it's not easy."

"What isn't easy?"

"What I have to say. But I'll say it quickly and get it over with, and then we can talk about what you did on your trip, and who you saw and what you said and what *they* said . . ."

"You never change," I said. "You just can't bring yourself to change. You're still a defensive colored girl from the States, and a hundred years in Paris and all the fancy men and modeling jobs won't change you."

She took a long time to say, "I thought maybe I was getting less that way. Maybe it will be better in a year or two. I've decided to stay, you know."

"I thought maybe you had."

"I'm no less radical because I'm living well," she said.

"I see your hair's still short, if that's what you mean."

"It's far beyond that," she said. "But I don't want to talk about it. There's something else . . ." She ran her fingers along the metal curves of the chair.

"Say it," I said, trying to keep my voice even. A woman with a shabby uniform had come over to us to ask for the ten-franc rental of the chairs.

"Let *me*," said Olivia grandly as I pushed her hand away, paid for the tickets, and tried to keep the train of thought. "Say it," I repeated crossly.

"Well, okay. I'll say the whole thing. Remember one afternoon, when I first came to Paris?"

"The day of the picnic?"

"No, in those first days when everything seemed so wonderful. Well, of course you wouldn't remember. But I planned that day, *that day* I wouldn't, ah, take any precautions, on purpose, because I wanted, ah, I wanted . . ."

"What, for Christ's sake. You wanted *what?*"

"A BABY!" she shouted. "I wanted us to have a baby! Do you want me to spell it out? I thought it would make us grow up, make us happy. That's why I was so sick with those cramps before I went to Switzerland. Don't you see that's why I told you to go off on your trip. *There was no Raf*. I went to Geneva alone! I spent our last miserable weeks together trying to decide. Now you're going to say 'decide what?' "

"No, I'm not going to say 'decide what?' I guess I can figure it out," I said in a quiet voice.

"I decided not to have it. It was an important decision

for me. We aren't ready for it and we probably never will be ready for it, so I had to get rid of it and now it's over. It's all over. And you'll tell me I'm being maudlin if I say it's all over just like the summer," she added, kicking some leaves at her feet. "And I'm not going to cry about it, so don't worry about having to console me."

"What about *me?*" I said. "Who's going to console *me?*"

"*You?*" she cried. "Still *you*. Everything still revolves around *you!*"

I said, after pounding the seat with my fist, that I had hoped maybe I was getting less that way too, after having been in Europe all that time and having all those experiences. It ought to have made one's own importance less, somehow.

Olivia looked at me. It was a worldly look. I turned away, embarrassed by my speech.

I mumbled, "It wasn't *Europe*. It was something that happened just these last weeks, when I was alone. I don't really know what it was. Maybe I'll never find out."

Then after a while in a small voice, and very much out of character, Olivia said, "Do you think we'll ever grow up?"

We sat far apart, staring at a small model schooner drifting toward the far shore of the pond where it was picked up by its middle-aged owner, who stooped with difficulty to turn it around and put it out to sea once again.

After I returned to America, I lost touch with Olivia for a long while. Once, when Jacobson came to New York he called me, and we spent an awkward hour at the outdoor café of the St. Moritz trying to think of things to say. He enjoyed gossip, and halfway through the conversation he

managed to tell me that Olivia had married a Frenchman
with a very expensive last name, never came near the Mars
Club, and was living in great style near the Bois de
Boulogne. I did pick up a copy of *Paris-Match* one day in
a dentist's office in Lyons, and there was a blurry photograph of Olivia dancing at the annual *Bal* at Monte Carlo.
Then I lost track of her until once in the New York *Daily
News* in January of 1962 there was a very clear picture of
her sitting at a counter in Woolworth's, taken in Huntsville, Alabama. Her hair now formed a perfect topiary
hedge around her wonderful face. The caption read:
"Sit-ins again go calmly in the South," and the short article
said that "a small group of Negroes sat at a luncheon
counter at Woolworth's in Huntsville, ignored by the
waitress and other store personnel. There were no distur-
bances and no arrests." Olivia, I noted, had gained a little
weight, and on the counter in front of her were a few
books, one of which she was extravagantly attempting to
study.

I called the office of CORE for her address and eventually they gave it to me. When my letter reached her, she
called.

"I had this *feeling* I'd hear from you," she began, and
after we went through all that, she sprung instantly on my
first question. I needed only to ask about Paris, and what
had happened to her view of the Eiffel Tower and her
count.

"We were annulled!" she said in triumph. "By the Vatican itself. Oh, I got so *bored* with him. We never *talked*
about anything."

"You probably never gave him a chance," I said. "I'd almost forgotten . . ."

"Well, as soon as I'm finished with this story, you'll

have *your* chance. Anyway, I realized that husbands and wives don't *talk* to each other in Europe the way they do here. I mean, I never really knew what he *did!* I would kiss him on the cheek each morning, standing in the front hall of that rambling apartment on the Victor Hugo, and say, 'Have a nice day, darling, doing whatever it is that you *do* do.' So we just dwindled down to nothing."

I never learned about her connection to the sit-ins. She suddenly had a call waiting on another line, so we hung up, promising to keep in touch, but the next time I heard from Olivia it was an unlikely postcard from Niagara Falls, saying, "I'm married again. Here's looking at you, kid."

The night train from the South of France arrives in Paris at around seven in the morning. I was on a trip from Provence to Brussels, required to change trains at the Gare de Lyon. I obediently got off the train, hoping to get through Paris as quickly as possible, figuring that on this cold February morning it would only depress me. But then all at once, and without reason, standing in front of the station, I decided that I needed to replace the celestial chart I had bought long ago at a shop near the Place Vendôme. It was a cardboard disk of deep blue, I remembered, showing the constellations as they appeared from various places on the earth at various times of the year. At that moment, the eternal stars, the circular chart, the musty store, and the city itself coalesced, and I knew I must remain in Paris for one night or maybe two, missing my connecting train. Exhaling with resignation, I looked left, in the early-morning gloom, for a taxi. I was advised by the signs to stand in line and I obliged. When my turn came I eased myself into the taxi with a smile of gratitude

that passed unnoticed by its lady driver, her steel-rimmed
glasses glinting with skepticism. On hearing the address of
a hotel I dredged up from another time, she repeated it
sternly, allowing me an ossified nod. On the car radio, Piaf
sang that she regretted nothing, neither the good nor the
bad, no, nothing, nothing at all.

We began to move slowly through the early-morning
traffic. I realized that a German shepherd was seated next
to the driver when it picked up its head and threw me a
baleful glance. A policeman blew his whistle, stopping us
with majesty just as we reached the Pont-Royal; then,
touching his cap with a salute, he waved us on without
apology. The driver quickly hissed at a slow-going car,
reprimands dancing in her head. And all the while Piaf,
game Piaf, dead for almost two decades, vibrated still. I
looked out at the cold beautiful streets and wondered, as I
feared I would, given the good and the bad of Paris,
whether I should have long ago capitulated and chosen
never to live anywhere else.

The hotel, near the Odéon, had remained grime-covered
even after all the polishing under Malraux. Most of its current tenants were desultory foreign students, too pale and
too thin. A phone booth had been wedged into the land-
ing, and at all hours they drifted up and down the thread-
bare staircase waiting for calls, carrying small parcels of
what looked like food, and no books. Each time I passed
the phone, someone was saying into the receiver that he or
she hated Paris and wanted to go home, and that yes, oh
yes, they were certainly free to be taken out for a meal.

It frequently happens when I feel myself a stranger in a
known place that the loss of familiar things begins to tyr-
annize me. The chestnut trees along the boulevards were
now leafless, the metal chairs in the Tuileries were empty;

SELF cafeterias now blinked shamelessly on street corners once occupied by straightforward bistros. A boutique-strewn shopping center now occupied part of the vast, empty lot left from the debris of my beloved Halles. In Beaubourg a brash new museum squatted, exposing its plumbing in primary colors. No one strolled or dawdled, no one flirted or seemed to speak. Even the sky remained uncompromisingly leaden, a formless concierge withholding from Paris the welcome delivery of a snowfall. But I was complaining too much and I had just arrived. Complaint, as everyone knows, is France's great contagion.

I left the hotel before unpacking, much to the proprietor's surprise, unable to conceive of paying for something unused. Crossing the river once again, I checked into the Ritz.

I found the small stuffy store without difficulty. In its small upstairs room I was handed the celestial chart. It was just as I had remembered it. An elderly man who had been examining a telescope came over to stand next to me as the clerk explained, as patiently as he could, how to line up the several spheres within the circle.

"You have a telescope?" asked the old gentleman when the salesman had left me to figure out the rest of it for myself. I said that no, I hadn't.

"You ought to have one. You ought to see the stars one at a time. Each one has its own brilliance. Then when you look at the sky you no longer see it the same way you had seen it before."

He waited a minute to let that sink in. I saw that in his buttonhole he wore the discreet ribbon of some august *légion* and I wondered which one it was.

"Each single thing is much more interesting than the

whole," he added with emphasis, distractedly stroking his large nose.

I told him that I agreed, that although I'd always seen my life that way I sometimes considered it a serious mistake.

"Never!" he said sharply, moving away toward the telescopes.

When I left the shop with my package I wondered about the conversation, and why I was tempted to personalize such cosmic theories with a stranger. But this reflection was cut short when I thought I saw Olivia turning a corner. It was her shoulder bag that caught my eye. Large leather pouches had always particularized her, as though at any moment she might be called away for a sudden trip. The assurance, too, was hers.

"Olivia!" I called in gratitude, in despair, stricken all at once by nostalgia. The figure turned. She squinted to take me in.

"I *knew* it, I *knew* it, I *knew* it!" she said. In the past she had repeated things only once.

We rushed toward each other in a transparent tunnel of twenty years.

"I'm not surprised," I said, as she said, at the same time, "Something *told* me I'd run into you. Oh, wonderful, wonderful. Oh, how time has flown."

Then there was a long minute while we stood still.

"Paris" was all I said, and as the chill winds drew our hands back into our pockets, we kept studying each other, trying to remember Paris as we wanted to think it had been for us.

"Let's not talk about the change," I said finally.

"How we've changed?" said Olivia. "Well, we wouldn't

have recognized each other"—she smiled—"if we'd changed *that* much."

I said, "I meant Paris."

"Well, to *me*, it's just a big, fantastic, ah, *majestic* city now, without magic. A place to do business. Actually, I'm here for a convention, a conference on—I know this will make you laugh, because you always laughed at my interest in the *occult*—a conference on Psychic Disclosures. And—you'll never believe this—I *knew* I'd run into you! It's amazing! It's just amazing! We went to the cemetery yesterday to the tomb of a psychic, a *famous* psychic you never heard of, named Alan Kardel. It's the most popular tomb at Père-Lachaise. His bust is all bright and shiny from everyone *touching* it as they ask for favors. And all his followers bring flowers. They're not crazy people, as you might think."

"It's amazing," I said, standing there, jostled by the passersby on the narrow sidewalk of the rue de l'Echelle. "I haven't seen you in almost twenty years and you're already telling me what I think. You've got to be the most exasperating woman I've ever known."

She sighed, pretending to adjust the flap on her pocketbook. I noticed the small lines around her eyes and a slight puffiness underneath them. Even with her bulky coat, I could tell that her tall body had filled out, though she was too voluptuous to be matronly. But she now took up more space, had more authority. She had become, I thought, a genuine figure. Everyone looked at her in passing, and not only because she was beautiful.

"We're already fighting," she said, looking hurt. "Aren't you glad we didn't get married and have lots of children and you'd find yourself stuck with me the rest of your life?"

"I am glad," I said, cupping her chin in my hand, thinking that with all her talk about growing up she had probably never managed it. "Now, what I'd really like to know is what *you* asked for, standing at that tomb, the wind howling down the crumbling roads of that stark place . . ."

"Goodness, you've gotten poetic . . ."

"You've come all the way to Paris and I'll bet you still manage to stay away from the Louvre. Instead, you're up there at Père-Lachaise, bypassing the tombs of Chopin and Piaf," I persisted, half-joking, realizing midway that she was serious. "And so, there you stood, next to the polished bust of a psychic, feeling . . ."

"Solemn. I was *solemn*. And *believing*. If I didn't have faith in the man I would never have gone to his tomb. Some very fancy people were there waiting on line . . ."

"*Believing*," I repeated, sorry I'd made fun. I imagined Olivia approaching the monument swiftly, in the forest of grey stones, a vermilion rose in her hand.

"What did you ask for?"

"I asked for South America," said Olivia.

I took a long look at her.

"I'm sick of coming to Europe and not being thrilled. I want to try South America. And *Rio* has never seen anything like *me*."

I was about to reply, but Olivia discovered, with a theatrical whoop, that she was late for her afternoon seminar and we quickly made a date for dinner.

I walked across the Tuileries, past the small boat basin where so many years ago Olivia and I had last seen each other. The chairs were all empty now, and the small puddles in the basin had frozen. I was relieved to find the Jeu de Paume still open. Trying hard not to think about past-present things, and the overall, nagging suspicion that nothing about us ever really changes except our surroundings, I knew I would find only pleasure inside that gallery. Nothing dark and incomprehensible cloaks those canvases; there are no universal truths. The glinting fields and choppy seas refreshed me, and by the time I left the gallery it was already dark and it had begun to snow.

When I turned the corner onto the Place Vendôme, all the lights were out. The cars circled around it with caution, and a frazzled policeman tried to direct the traffic leading to the lighted rue de Rivoli. Inside the Ritz there were candles on every surface. Everything was muted, muffled; from beyond the lobby a violin played Fauré's *Ballade*, and for a long moment the place was transported, taking me with it to a time I never knew, with Proust entering the lobby late in the evening to have his raspberry sherbet after dining with friends. And following that sudden vision, I thought in the candlelight of earlier images, of Maupassant's Paris, the Paris of Balzac, of Restif de La Bretonne . . . It was disappointing when a few minutes later the lights went on and the candles were removed.

How would this present Paris be remembered a long time from now?

Olivia and I met on the rue Pierre-Charron at Joseph's, a restaurant glistening with mirrors and paneling and good china. Olivia made an entrance, late, of course, wearing furs and a turban.

"You are spectacular as you always were," I said when we were seated. "And not at all the way you looked in the picture at a Woolworth's lunch counter in Alabama."

"Yes," she said. "That was when we were all stirred up about *power to the people*. I was very serious about that. I mean, *very* serious. I've tried, since then, to remember exactly what we imagined would happen in America if all our hopes and dreams were to come true. I'll have a martini, please," she said to the waiter who stood above us in his crisp uniform. "I mean an iced gin martini, not a glass of vermouth. So often in Europe," she said in an undertone, "they get it wrong."

"Things have changed," I said. "Twenty years ago we were scratching around Times Square trying to find a restaurant to give us a table. Now you're telling them how you like your martinis."

"We were always privileged people," she said, waving away the comment. "We might not have realized it until we got to Europe. But they sure loved us when we got here."

"Then," I said, "they sure loved us then."

Olivia continued, "So much happened in the middle. Everything seemed to shift. You know, I got very disenchanted with the movement, long after that incident at Woolworth's. I think it was in '72. By then I was hanging around with the Black Muslims. There was a bad brawl on the streets. A white TV photographer got beaten up and kicked by our group, not a bad group, really, but they suddenly turned into savages. No one could stop them. They threw rocks. The man hadn't *done* anything. It was terrible. Terrible! After so much, ah, progress, to see such wasteful anger. The photographer turned into a *vegetable* before my eyes. I couldn't get it out of my mind. I left them all a few days later—in Baton Rouge, it was—and came on my own back East. I never went back into the movement. It was all over for me then, I guess."

"And what about your husband? Remember, Niagara Falls, and 'Here's looking at you, kid?'"

"Ah yes. Well, my husband, you see, was the one throwing the rocks."

Olivia looked around the beautiful room. "You and I never managed to come to places like this back then, not that it mattered. I finally got around to fancy restaurants with that first husband, the one I met just before you left Paris. But we've already talked about *him*." She smiled over the rim of her cocktail, her small finger extended horizontally. Her eyes then scanned the room again. "You see that woman over there? The one who's pretending not to be staring at us, not to be studying our every move? She's going to *come over to this table* and say, '*Aren't* you Miss Verrett?' Or 'Excuse me, Miss Price, but *your Tosca* was mag-nificent.' It happens all the time. Whenever I find myself in a really good restaurant, that is."

"It's probably what you want them to do."

She pondered this. "Well, I've never minded attention. But I'd much prefer it if it was for *me*. Wouldn't you?"

I said that I accepted attention wherever I found it.

"Just like the old days," we said, chiming our glasses together.

"But what I can't quite follow about you," I said, certain that it would capture her attention away from the woman on the banquette opposite (who was, in fact, preparing to cross the room to our table), "is that you gave up Paris, became a rebel, and then gave that up . . ."

"Well, frankly," she said in an aside, putting down her glass and leaning toward me, "I mean, this is a *thousand* percent for you. But I am going to be fifty, *fifty* in a year or two. And it's hard to be a rebel if you *grunt* when you get up from a chair."

We started to laugh, and Olivia had one of the knee-slapping, back-porch fits I had loved so much and almost forgotten. The waiter, taken by surprise, looked coolly in our direction and then, infected, smiled. And the woman from the other table, almost upon us, cautiously withdrew a foot or two.

"And so I went into the *consulting* business," she said between spasms, wiping the laughter tears from her eyes. "And I'm really quite a success at it! I mean, isn't that what people do, who *just can't get it together?*"

Slowly Olivia regained her composure. I watched the metamorphosis with some sadness, like seeing a perfect line drawing obscured by fine color. She drew her furs around her shoulders and removed from a small satin bag a pair of collapsible glasses. With her long fingers, she opened them at their hinges and put them into place, slowly, elegantly sliding the earpieces underneath her turban.

"And now," she said, picking up the menu. "Let's have a fan*tas*tic dinner. We are in Paris, after all. And with the possibility of Rio, who knows? We might *nevah* come back to Paris *evah* again."

The Sweet Life

E*cco, Roma,*" announced the hefty driver of my taxi fifteen years ago as we rounded a bend coming in from the airport. He stopped the car but kept the motor running. "This is the hill of the Gianicolo, and *that*"—he paused—"is Rome."

He said it with a trustee's pride. Behind us a massive fountain gushed shamelessly into a Renaissance basin big enough to bathe fifty.

"*Ah, Roma, Roma,*" he sighed, filling in my silence and well aware, in the wag of his head, of his own raffish charm. "Look at it!"

With a meaty palm he passed me the view, depositing it in the back seat with a flourish. I wanted to get out and see it properly, my first reasonable glimpse of the city, but as my hand reached for the door handle his foot hit the accelerator.

"*Ecco, Roma,*" repeated the flouncing young porter, forty minutes later, as he banged open the shutters against the *pensione*'s flaking façade. Then he stood aside to admire with sheep's eyes his own reflection in the mirror.

I looked out at the view, locating with difficulty the same Renaissance fountain where the taxi had stopped, now way in the distance on top of its hill, its waters glistening in the sunlight. It was within this sprawl, a city carved out of ancient cow paths, set between the Gianicolo and the Trinità dei Monti, between the primeval peasant's palm and the all-pervasive Roman vanity, that I was to live. The porter accepted his tip, flashing a smile that incorporated brilliant teeth, long lashes, ambiguous sexuality, and an enviable weightlessness of mind, all of it meant to be charming.

The charm, the charm, the charm! In restaurants babies were supposed to be charming when they crawled between your feet and dribbled on your ankles. Old men charmed, their pinkies pointing north as they drank their cappuccinos. Boys charmed, secure in their knowledge that the protruding element at the base of their torsos was the axis on which the entire world revolved. The girls charmed too; they knew, by the thirsting looks, the furtive feels, that no matter what their mirrors told them, they would be wanted, they would be married, they would be mothers.

Perhaps I am overstating it. In its society, as the levels grew loftier, as the carpets, so to speak, grew thicker, *charm* was more carefully apportioned, and malice began to show through, malice, I suppose, being the underbelly of charm. But let it pass, let it pass. In the sixties, almost everyone at every street corner still beamed, or so it seemed. And it was possibly the last time one could walk into the chrome-colored, deckle-edged picture postcard Italy was still pretending to be.

My first apartment was a walk-up above the Fontana di Trevi with a terrace overlooking the extravagant Trevi fountain, its Tritons, sea paraphernalia, and horses lunging out of the side of an otherwise undistinguished office building adjacent to mine. I remember the sound more clearly than the details of the fountain, for it was as though I was living next to a tideless, continuously crashing sea which all of a sudden, at two in the morning, would cease. The quiet then was as powerful as the sound, and frequently it would awaken me. Out of the now silent streets, Roman boys of about ten or eleven would miraculously appear, hopping like elves over the rim of the fountain, their shoes left behind on the paving stones, their trousers rolled up, searching as intently as pearl divers for coins tossed into the waters by foreigners who had heard from Hollywood that a coin in the fountain assured a return to Rome. Then the kids would gather dripping under the streetlamps, their negotiations echoing through the sleeping streets.

"Ethiopia. This one's from Ethiopia."

"*I mortacci tuoi*, a curse on your dead ones. It's not worth anything. I want to find some money from America."

"*America!*" The single word bounced off the Tritons and horses, across the now stilled pool, echoing upward in the star-filled night. *America*. It still had the ring of the promised land, it still seemed a million miles away and carved out of gold.

I stayed in the apartment only a few months and then its owner came back to town and I had to move. Through some friends I heard about a place on the Piazza Farnese recently vacated by an American woman. Whenever her name came up in conversation she was referred to as That Nymphomaniac.

Dressed carefully in a new suit to impress the landlords and staff, I sped to the Piazza Farnese to look at the apart-

ment. The *portiere* of the building, Angelo, wore his cap at
a rakish angle and stroked his bushy mustache. Seeing the
suit, he bowed low. I later discovered that he was the kind
of joke-Italian servant so often appropriated by librettists:
duplicitous, venal, a tattler and a snob. But he beamed with
smiles. His wife, a plump woman whose white hair was
pulled back into a peasant's bun, beamed as well. Only
later did I understand that she was clinically feebleminded.
Their son was also at the monumental palace door when I
got there. He did not beam. He twinkled. At sixteen he
had already committed himself to the deft use of cosmetics. I did not realize this, either. I thought that he had
particularly large brown eyes and a rosy complexion.

The apartment was perched like a small cottage on the
roof of the palazzo. The so-called nymphomaniac had left
behind only one object, appropriately a large lumpy bed. I
glanced around the bedroom in the sunlight screened
through the shutters, and in an unexpected cinematic
effect the sun gently withdrew, leaving the room and the
bed in darkness. Suddenly there was the sound of thunder,
and I went out to the terrace. It had begun to rain, an
early-autumn rain that might have been melancholy anywhere else. But Rome was so filled with promise that the
rain, scented with wood smoke and burnt espresso, signaled instead snug pleasures and long ardent nights. A
voice startled me.

"I always leave something behind. I've left most of my
life behind in other places. I've got a trunk and two suitcases in Paris somewhere. But that's Paris and that's over. I
left an entire medicine cabinet here, full of everything I
need. I've come back for it. I hadn't meant to startle you."

Because it was dark and there were no lamps, I could
not distinguish her face. I saw only the hands, restlessly

moving in the wan light from the terrace: long fingers with prominent joints; they seemed to be trying to mold her words into shapes.

"I couldn't quite hear you," I said, coming inside.

"I have what is called slurred speech." She moved toward the terrace door into the half-light.

She could never have been beautiful even at a younger age, even given the broad cheekbones. Her eyes were puffy and her face was extremely long, sculptured without care, the lank brown hair bordering it left to fall as it would. The striking effect was similar to those movie actresses of the black-and-white forties who tossed their heads, spoke in low, tough voices, and wore square-shouldered clothing.

"I'm Brenda Cloak," she said.

"Cloak," I repeated.

"Yes. It's an odd name. Cloak. Everything about me is, well, odd. I was born in Jamaica. Oh, not the Jamaica in Long Island. On a broken-down sugar plantation. Lots of shadowy rooms and mahogany furniture and peeling wallpaper and bamboo crowding outside. We thought of ourselves as colonials. Oh, we didn't stay there very long. But why am I telling you all this?" Then, turning her head, she shouted, "Benedetto! What are you up to?"

The sallow, somewhat elegant young man she summoned appeared from the bathroom carrying several bottles of pills. "I was looking through your inter-resting drug collection," he said with an aristocratic Piedmontese accent rolling in a sea of uvular *r*'s. "Some people collect good pictures, like my grandfather did. Some people collect . . ."

"This is Benedetto Sanmartino," interrupted Brenda Cloak. "I do not collect drugs, if that's what he is inferring. If I collect anything, I collect experiences. Roles. Back in America you can't do this so easily. You have to know exactly who you are. As soon as you meet someone they ask you, 'What do you *do?*' Here I feel so much, ah, roomier."

She paused for breath. Her voice was like a buzz saw and she barely opened her lips wide enough to be clearly understood.

"Here," she concluded, "you can be whatever you're in the mood to be. You *become* it."

"Like Pirandello," Benedetto observed.

"Benedetto was at the head of his class in Turin," said Brenda. "He has been filled with promise for ten or twelve years. I will not tell you how many years I myself have been filled with promise."

"Don't," said Benedetto, extending a thin hand to formalize their leaving.

"We've got to go now," said Brenda. "Idle people are always in a rush."

When they were halfway down the stairs Brenda turned and waved, smiling, for the first time. "You'll be happy here," she said. They clattered out. I signed the lease the next morning.

Soon after renting the small roost high above the piazza, I opened a photography studio around the corner on the Via Giulia, and so my spatial detachment was now reinforced by my profession: living high above the hectic streets and seeing Rome and my clients through lenses. I mention this to emphasize my isolation, a way of life, it seemed to me, altogether in harmony with the Rome of that time.

It was while I was at Cinecittà photographing an actress that I wandered into one of the studios where they were dubbing a film into English. A portion of the film was being projected onto a screen, a crowd scene in which a king and queen glided by in a fine carriage spattering mud on the unfortunates lining the road. The ill-assorted group gathered around the microphone were required to make crowd noises, various pitiful and unctuous cries of poverty. Among the assembled Americans lending their voices was Brenda Cloak.

"*Poorer,*" shouted the dubbing director as the same loop was projected again. "I want you to sound poorer and more miserable."

The scene was repeated, the foreigners groaned and pleaded, and in the midst of it all I saw, heard, Brenda cry out, "LIFE IS PAIN!"

The director stopped the film, walked over to Brenda, and grabbed her elbow.

"What do you think you're doing?" he said irritably. "I said *sounds,* not words."

"You're hurting my arm," she said through clenched teeth. "I was merely getting into the part."

"You are part of a crowd," he shouted. "You are only part of a crowd of poor people."

"That is what you might think," she said, releasing herself from his grasp. "I may be broke. But I am not *poor.*" Then she noticed me standing there and waved, the director signaled the projectionist, and they began once again.

Several days later the door to my studio opened and Brenda Cloak sidled in. She flung herself into a chair opposite my desk and lit a cigarette, muttering. I certainly could not have imagined that Brenda Cloak might have been a prospective client, given the way she looked, given her fuzzy-husky manner. Clearly she had come into my studio just to sit down on a chair. But those were the last

days before drugs began to seep into Italy and into all our
lives and we assumed that people were either drunk or
sober, and we still had difficulty identifying someone who
was stoned.

"I've just come from the river. I spent the night under a
bridge because Benedetto locked me out. It's a horrible
river, not at all like the Seine . . ." Her voice slid away
and she rubbed a bruise on her ankle.

"Imagine," she continued as I ordered us some coffee,
"spending the night under a bridge with nothing but
scrawny cats for company . . ." Her voice trailed off.
Then Brenda yawned, and I realized that the reason she
required herself to mumble and not to smile or laugh was
that her upper teeth were all missing, and the teeth she
wore had been fashioned out of some ersatz material that
made them look like celluloid.

"Now that you've ordered me some coffee," she said,
trying to sit up straight, "I ought to repay you with a few
anecdotes."

"No need . . ."

"Well, I mean, you asked me how I *was* when I came in
the door, and since each thing is tied to each other thing, it
is always a difficult question to answer. For example, my
ex-husband was over fifty when I married him and I was
twenty, just twenty, and just out of Bennington, precocious girl that I was. So that idiotic marriage is, in part, responsible for how I *am*, when someone asks, 'How are
you?'"

I cleared my throat.

"Well, why shouldn't I have married him? I was trying
to be a sculptor and he promised me Paris! He was rich, of
course, though I always wondered about the source of his
income. As much as one wonders about such things at

twenty!" She chuckled to herself. Then, abruptly, she said with venom, "He was actually a brutal and evil man and I had to leave him almost at once. For one thing"—and here she began to laugh—"he owned an entire wardrobe of women's undergarments! Why are you looking at me, studying me, I mean?"

The quick, drugged, changing angers and amusements were intriguing to me. Also, there was something touching about her fake toughness. I knew that in Rome, foreigners were expected to protect each other, help each other out. By taking care of someone, you insured yourself against the day you were certain to be in trouble yourself. Only a few of us had an actual address we could call our own. No job was more than temporary. If you turned someone down, this refusal would one day work against you. It was a fine pagan philosophy and it has kept southern Italy relatively free from the Christian ethic of doing good for its own sake. I heard myself sigh with a mixture of exasperation and inevitability. In one of those unsolicited moments of truth, I knew that something would have to be done about Brenda Cloak. Like it or not, she had slouched into my life.

"You've certainly managed to overcrowd your life with images," I said, looking at the wreck before me.

"Oh, one's life is so *episodic!*" She paused. "*Now* I see why you're looking at me so carefully. You noticed my, ah, my ghastly teeth. Don't say no. I don't blame you. My husband had my teeth knocked out in Paris one night on the Montagne Ste.-Geneviève as I left a bar. I lost the replacements. These"—she pointed a long finger toward her lips—"were made in Fez. Don't look so gloomy. There's no need to feel sorry for me. I'm a survivor, as you can see."

"Still," I said slowly, "it must be hard not to be able to let yourself laugh."

"It's lucky," she remarked after a long while, "that to live in Rome and find it beautiful, and even"—she turned her head away and laughed—"and even be a part of the Dolce Vita, I don't have to depend on my smile."

It seems strange now to write about the Dolce Vita, the Sweet Life, as much an artifact of that era as Fanfani's Opening to the Left. My friends used to come to Rome asking to be shown the Dolce Vita as though it was a national monument, like the Forum. But like most people living in Rome, I presumed that it was a harmless attitude giving the impression of pagan Rome and nothing bad ever came out of it. I was wrong, as it turned out.

My credentials for membership in the Dolce Vita set were modest. I avoided the Via Veneto, the assumed focal point of the louche Roman life, for among other things it was one of the few fake-fashionable, unbeautiful streets in the city. But every now and then I stayed up all night or walked barefoot in a fountain, or found myself at a party in a falling-apart palazzo. I was therefore pleased when Brenda and Benedetto invited me to one of their parties, this one on New Year's Eve.

The party was to take place in a boarded-up villa at Terracina, a summer resort outside of Rome. It was bitter cold that evening; high winds funneled down from the Abruzzi and snow was predicted. On New Year's Eve in Rome the custom was to throw bottles, glasses, anything breakable—chairs and tables as well—out of the windows and from rooftops: lopsided baby cribs and dead light bulbs flew past shuttered windows at midnight and only the adventurous, the cars, and the cats, picked their way across the glittering cobblestones.

I drove cautiously out of the city, and once on the open road moved swiftly past the phantom buildings of EUR to Ostia, where I pulled over and parked. The wind howled around the car as I got out and walked along the beach. Like so many others, I am most at home next to the sea. And even though the sea outside Rome is sluggish, and the sand is muddy and black, it made little difference to me. After all, it was the Mediterranean. One lone fishing boat glowed in the icy night, but I was already cynical enough to realize that it must have been carrying contraband cigarettes, at that hour, and not fish. The relative innocence of it pleased me. Crime in Italy seemed always on such a small, manageable level (as did everything else except the art and architecture).

I sat in the shelter of a dune and lit a cigarette, thinking that I was very snug in Rome, that coming to Italy—even allowing for the lure of its exceptional artifacts—was fundamentally a pursuit of good will, a spiritual trust in the land. These fine thoughts were nicely counterbalanced by the erotic images constantly spawned by the city. Finally, chilled, I returned to my car, and with the advance-retreat feelings I have always had about every party, I took a deep breath and headed for Terracina.

The villa was on a deserted street a block from the sea. Nothing moved except the dead leaves and the bits of paper skidding along the sidewalk. The shutters of the house had been closed, allowing only the thinnest strips of light to shine through.

The first thing that struck me inside the house were the out-of-season flowers. Vases filled with the tallest of

French lilacs, lilies, and almond blossoms crowded the corners of the living room.

"Yes," said Brenda, following my gaze, "Benedetto is incredibly extravagant. He's bought me this new dress as well," she added, dropping an angular curtsy before moving on.

"I hear you've sent Brenda to get some new teeth," said Benedetto in an undertone.

I said, "I have a friend who's a dentist."

"We all try to help, I guess," he said. "She's still staying with me in Trastevere. I seem to be operating a home for wayward foreigners."

I said, "You're generous. Brenda's told me that. She's very grateful."

He shrugged. "You see that kid over there? He's another one. He's with the Warhol factory. They fed him pills and got him to make a film without clothing. That is the trend nowadays."

I looked over at a rangy, boyish American who was talking with hectic intensity to a beautiful spaced-out girl. Her expression indicated that she was trying without success to lip-read what he was saying.

"Stark naked?" I said.

"I find it incr-redible that you don't keep up with what's going on. All these beautiful people popping pills, as they say, dressing up however they want, not worrying about what people think, staying out late or never coming home. They're free. They're grasshoppers, fiddling away while people like you, who are too serious, simply toil."

"I have my moments," I said, disturbed and somewhat envious and wondering whether I should be back in New York going crazy like everyone else.

"I'm cr-razy about Americans. They do what they want

to do. But they stay innocent. When they come to Europe they think they can live on air. Like that guy Love over there. Now that he's made a movie he thinks he can be a director. Hey, Love!" Benedetto called. "Say hello to another American."

I glanced over again at the young American, who looked as though he ought to be riding a horse across a prairie in Wyoming instead of speeding on drugs at a party in a boarded-up summer house outside of Rome.

"Hello, partner," he said amiably. "Isn't this house *great!* With the beach just down the street and the sea right there. You know the first thing that came into my mind when I saw the sea? Salinger!"

He waited a beat for me to register surprise, and I did.

His eyes lit up. "I've been trying to tell this girl his story about the banana fish. You know it? Well," he continued at a clip, waiting for neither a yes nor a no, "It's about this veteran, a young guy all messed up by the war. And he's on vacation, on a beach, and there's this little girl who wants to go in swimming, but she's afraid. So he takes her into the water. Now comes the *great* part. In order to calm her, he makes up a story about banana fish, and she gets so interested in them that she forgets to be afraid, and finally she thinks she actually *sees* them. This makes the veteran so happy that for one minute he manages to forget his own reality, his own miseries . . ."

Hugging Love as she passed, Brenda said with affection, "*Miseries* is not a word meant for your vocabulary. Now, what is this story?"

"I can't tell it again," said Love, collapsing back onto the sofa, where the beautiful girl removed a partridge-feather earring, pinched her earlobe, and placed his shaggy head against her.

"We took mescaline last night," said Benedetto with evident pride. "Brenda was obsessed. She spent the whole time sculpting. Love disappeared. And—I know this sounds insane—but all evening I kept weeping over a fifteenth-century painting of Christ. I never thought of the crucifixion before as an embracing, you see, I always thought of it as a symbol of mortal agony. I know, I know, it has nothing to do with this party, nothing to do with New Year's Eve. You'll say I'm trying to be clever and show how bright I am . . ."

I said, "Which fifteenth-century painting . . . ?"

"Jennifer wants to go swimming," interrupted Brenda.

"She's crazy," I said. "It's winter."

"He says you're crazy," said Brenda to a blond girl built like a full-blown peony, with rosy cheeks and good padding. I looked at her carefully and I guessed that the sea would not harm her at all.

"He is quite possibly *right*," said Jennifer, mightily British. "But the water is *there*. And it's only a block away, and it's meant to be *used*. You might think I'm *stoned* but I'm not. I shall go there fully clothed, unfasten everything, and *submerge* myself for one perfect moment. And no one will stop me."

"Have a smoke," said Brenda. "If you don't, it will be like driving in slow-motion onto a thruway where everyone's zooming past you at seventy miles an hour."

"Funny," I said. "I thought of it the other way around." I said this squinting through one of Benedetto's special reefers as we scuttled out of the door.

The cold wind picked up the sand, whirling it in our faces. The sea, here, was rougher. From far away I heard the sound of a bell, a church bell, I thought, from some phantom church in this deserted place, tolling the midnight mass for its spectral worshippers. But then in the darkness, between the crashing tides. I realized that it was a buoy way out beyond the curve of the coast.

Benedetto said, "You don't approve of us, do you." It was not a question.

I tried to keep my voice even. "Well, I'm here on the beach along with the rest of you."

"I don't mean necessarily just now."

"Look," I began, "I didn't come here to criticize. Maybe I find it hard to be a part of things. Let's just let it go at that."

"You mean, you're not just a foreigner to Italy," he said, putting his hand on someone's head to steady himself while he removed his elegant moccasins. "You're just a professional foreigner to everything. No offense meant, of course."

"An observer," I said, crediting him, inwardly, for shrewdness.

All at once Jennifer removed her coat, her dress, slip, bra, panties, and ran into the water with whooping cries of shock and pleasure. Then Brenda quickly followed, then others; then Love, who struggled to take off his western boots, fell, picked himself up, and ran, wearing his boots still, into the water.

"Well, all right," I said, unbuttoning my shirt and my blue jeans. "If you call this going seventy miles an hour . . ."

I can still see the semicircle of palely lit figures in the sea as I plunged in and swam toward them. In my mind they bob farther and farther away as I approach them until they disappear beyond the horizon. But I clearly remember Love swimming over to me determined to finish his story. He said, "What I wanted to tell you was that when the little girl said goodbye and ran down the beach, the veteran went back to his hotel room, took out an automatic, and shot himself." He gulped down a mouthful of water and shivered with the cold. "Excuse me for holding on to you," he said, "but I never really learned how to swim back in Arizona."

I said, "What's your first name, anyway?"

"No one ever uses it," he said, "ever since just *Love* was on the film credits. A lot of those guys took names. But mine's real."

I was beginning to feel numb with the cold. "It's more than a name," I said, smiling. "It's a responsibility." Then I moved toward the shore. None of us could have stayed in that freezing water any longer, and we quickly ran across the sand, half-entangled in our clothing, teeth chattering, back to the house.

Midnight passed with barely a murmur. When I look back on that evening I can see the dozen or so of us in the wavering candlelight, the December–January winds howling outside that summertime house. What surprises me, no, shocks me, is that the atmosphere inhabited by that relatively simple group of carefully bred kids, all with a vision of Italy as a land of sensual pleasures, would be so assaulted within a year.

The evening evolved into its own improvisation of the Sweet Life. I went slowly into one of the rooms of the villa, its floor gritty with the previous summer's sand, and on a crowded bed bereft of sheets, in the dimmest light, a disembodied hand beckoned to me like a single comma in a bulky paragraph.

The supper—lentils and sausages, the New Year's Eve tradition—was never served. When I surveyed the living room one last time, at dawn, I noticed that all the extravagant flowers had fallen into limp attitudes of beseechment. The generous Benedetto had neglected to put water in their containers. I threaded my way into the kitchen past the mute figures on the sofas, the heaped ashtrays, past the coagulating stews on the stove, but there was no sign of a pitcher. I found instead an empty garbage pail and filled it with water. It could not have helped those flowers much by then. The streets sparkled with broken glass and I got home without a flat tire as the wan sun rose on that chilly January day.

It was a foreigner's habit to get caught up with acquaintances for a while, and then, because everything was so transient, move on to something else. So I became a part of that self-styled Dolce Vita band, or as much a part of it as my non-joining nature would allow. They formed and re-formed like an amoeba, absorbing and rejecting new faces. I notice that I write *they* and not *we*, which is how I must have seen us then.

My studio on the Via Giulia made me easily accessible to anyone with time on his hands to stop by for a chat, though luckily I began to be too busy with paying customers to listen long. And so we saw each other for occasional evenings and outings throughout that winter and spring. Jennifer played the cello at the Gonfalone, a baroque oratory off the Via Giulia. Love signed up for a course at Cinecittà, Benedetto bought and sold eighteenth- and nineteenth-century drawings—mostly to relatives—and Brenda sculptured in wax. Every now and then she would sell something through a gallery, and with the money she would move away from Benedetto's apartment to a *pensione*. But she usually went back within a month.

Someone—I cannot remember which one of us—discovered a sulfur spring north of Rome which must have dated back to Etruscan times, and we drove there late at night when the weather got warm, up the Via Aurelia toward Civitavecchia, turning down a hidden dirt road, past ruined stone houses overgrown with vines, and then—unexpectedly, each time a surprise—we came upon an uneven rock pool. Steam rose from the warm waters, and hidden by night, we slid into the spring, the mud at the bottom oozing between our toes.

Brenda held my hand to steady herself getting into the warm pool, quite regal under the moonlight, her free hand raised, an entrance as grand as Salacia's might have been, descending to meet Neptune. Her teeth had finally been replaced, and now, from time to time, she hazarded an open smile.

"Brenda is the first hippie in Rome," said Love from the shadows.

"What is a hippie?" asked Brenda.

"It is something we read about in an English magazine," said Benedetto, always the first with things. "Like a beatnik."

"I detest categories," said Brenda, fully submerged.

"That's why you're a hippie," said Heather, a sloe-eyed young girl who then vanished under the water, reappearing with handfuls of mud which she applied with voluptuous caresses to her breasts and shoulders.

"This immersing ourselves is like a rite," said Love, standing next to me, waist high in the hot water. Everything he did or said seemed to imply a new, important, and profound discovery, though it was difficult not to credit Benedetto's drugs for supplying the intensity.

I said, "Some things just are what they are. This is a sulfur spring on a hill above the Mediterranean, and we come here on a moonlit night to enjoy ourselves. Isn't that enough?"

"That's how you see it," he said, lowering himself into the water up to his chin and then back up again, his body glistening.

I shrugged.

"*I* see everything as a privilege," he continued. "Ever since I left home, all the things that have happened to me, making movies in New York, coming to Italy. Everything in my life has a special meaning. My whole life's a high!" He rubbed his hands up and down his chest. "I feel as though I have been singled out."

"Maybe you're lucky," I said, digging my feet into the mud. "Maybe I've always taken too much for granted."

"Maybe I'm just more special than you are," he said grinning, pouncing on my neck to pull me under the water.

Suddenly, from the high branches of a tree overhead, a nightingale began to sing. It was so startling and unexpected that we were silenced at once. The enchanting oboe-like solo rose above the Etruscan hills, tempting all of us with an accidental spiritual reverie.

"How can you explain that?" whispered Love. "How can you take that for granted?"

As if in defiance I heard myself begin to say that it was almost unbearable, all of it. But the vapors rising from the pool would have none of such talk; neither would the healthy, sensual bodies surrounding me, the too-round moon above, nor the immaculate sound emerging from some invisible source in the treetops.

I slid slowly and silently into the warmth of the water and whispered to whoever wanted to hear it, "After all, I am very, very happy . . ."

And before I could recant, other lips—velvet, they seemed —covered mine, and the water flowed into my ears obscuring the fugitive melody.

I have never heard such iridescent notes again. I tried not long ago to retrace the path leading to those warm springs, but either the hidden road has become overgrown with bushes and wildflowers or the pool has dried up, but I could no longer find it.

In Hollywood films of the thirties and forties the passage of time was often shown by using a calendar with large numerals, its pages riffled by a powerful off-camera wind: January gives way to February, and so on until all at once everything is still, the date is different, and all the actors have gone attractively grey. So many images of Rome are cinematic that the fleeing calendar pages come easily to mind when recalling that time. I know that in November of that year both Venice and Florence were hit by bad floods, and many of us drove up in trucks to Florence to help shovel some of the sludge from the shores of the Arno. Brenda stayed on there to work with the restorers, glad to have a purpose for a while.

But I cannot remember exactly when I read in the Roman newspaper that a young American named Dennis Lowe was found unconscious on the Via Condotti in the early hours of the morning. It might have been six months after the evening of the nightingale. But everyone connected to the incident is gone. Brenda has long ago disappeared, Jennifer slimmed down and married an earl, and Benedetto is dead. I had tried in all that time to keep aloof from the group and I thought I had succeeded, but I didn't stand a chance.

It was a short article on an inside page of *Il Messaggero*.

"Dennis Lowe, a young American, was found unconscious in the early hours of the morning on the Via Condotti. He was brought to the emergency room of San Giovanni, where the poor boy, *il proverino*, lapsed into a coma and died."

I had been drinking my morning coffee when I read the story. I put the cup down, missed the saucer, and spilled the coffee onto my lap and the carpet in my unheated living room. I remember this because during the next half hour I was aware of the dampness spreading over my shirt and trousers, externalizing my fears. I telephoned the American Embassy. No one, it seemed, had heard of Dennis Lowe; no one had read anything but the Rome *Daily American* that morning. I left my phone number and hung up. Then I put on my coat and ran outside, crossing the Ponte Sisto into Trastevere. One of Benedetto's eccentricities was that he had no telephone. He finally came to the door.

"What time is it?" he asked, yawning powerfully.

"Look, Benedetto, I . . ."

"Come on in," he said.

I stayed in the doorway. "Is Love here?"

He shook his head no. Then he choked back another yawn. "He goes out a lot. Sometimes he doesn't come home."

I said, "Like this morning?"

"Yes."

He walked to his desk, tripping on the belt from his bathrobe. "I have a bad hangover."

"Was Love's name Dennis?" I had the newspaper open to the article.

He nodded sleepily.

"Jesus," I said.

There was a long pause. I could feel the anger growing. "Wake up!" I shouted. "You tell me you're running a home for waywards, but under all that high-class aristocratic polish you're playing around with low-down things you know nothing about. What drugs did you give Love?"

"What are you so angry about?" he said.

"I'm angry because you've been filling that kid and everyone else with drugs. You never understood the danger."

"Aren't you Mr. Per-r-fect," he mocked. "*Signore Perfetto*. It is what we always call you. Always so careful, so good, so responsible." He was sneering. "Always staying out of trouble."

I heard myself say very quietly, "You've killed him, you careless son of a bitch."

There was no sound. I could not take the words back.

"Something has happened," I said finally, trying to control myself. I held the paper out to him.

As though propelled onto a stage, he swiftly crossed the room and had the newspaper in his hand.

"You've got to . . ." I began, not knowing what I was going to say.

He had finished reading it. With both hands he grabbed me around the neck and brought my head down sharply. His face was sweaty and his breath was sour. His mouth was next to my ear. "Go!" he whispered hoarsely. His fingers dug into my shoulders.

"What was it?" I shouted. "What did he take?"

"It was Seconal, it was dope, it was a bottle of brandy. What do you care what it was?"

Then he pushed himself free of me and moved to another door. When he turned around his face was chalk-white.

"GO AWAY!" he shouted. "GO HOME BEFORE YOU'RE CONTAMINATED, YOU SMUG BAS-TARD!"

When I came into my living room I found two detectives there.

"*Dottore*," said the one without the uniform, inclining his head with unspecified deference.

When Romans give false titles they either want something from you or believe you to be rich.

"Your housekeeper was kind enough to let us in. The American Embassy gave us your name. You called them, it seems, concerning Dennis Lowe. They know very little about him and so do we. This is a most charming view of the Palazzo Farnese. Most people think that the entire design of the palazzo is by Michelangelo, but in fact it is only just the cornice opposite you. One could say you have your own private Michelangelo. The inspector has Dennis Lowe's passport. We were hoping you might be helpful."

The uniformed inspector handed me the passport without a word. On its second page, Dennis Love was pictured, perched on a photographer's stool in Phoenix with a broad smile, imagining Europe.

"Love," I corrected. "Not Lowe."

"We have no *w* in the Italian alphabet," said the man who had spoken of Michelangelo. "So we confuse it with a *v*."

"That was the one chance," I muttered, "that it might have been a mistake."

"He was found unconscious," said the man in uniform. "He had drunk too much. They brought him to the hospital to sleep it off. He slept it off all right. A good-looking

guy, and young. What a waste. You Americans throw
yourselves away. Soon you'll teach it to us."

"You Italians are careless in other ways," I said. "If your
quack doctors had bothered to pump his stomach instead
of leaving him . . ."

"I think drugs are involved, from the report, *dottore*. I
repeat, we would like to know more about his life in
Rome," he said, tapping a wooden figure I had brought
back from Egypt. "Authentic, authentic and appropriate.
This is Anubis," he observed to the other inspector. "It is
the dog of ancient Egypt who watches over the dead."

"Ah, yes," said the inspector with feigned interest and a
heavy sigh.

"I don't know very much," I began, knowing I was no
good at lying. "I wish I could help, which is why I called
the Embassy."

Frequently when I am nervous I begin to stutter, and
the refinements of language are unavailable to me. I knew
this, and I tried to say as little as possible. I also knew that
once an investigation was begun everyone connected to
Love would be in serious trouble. Foreigners were thrown
out of Italy in twenty-four hours if there was any hint of
drugs.

"I know where he had most of his meals," I said. "The
waiters there all knew and l-liked him. A place called the
Re degli Amici on . . ."

". . . the Via della Croce. That is a good beginning.
Waiters and *portieri* are often reliable. And who is Brenda
Cloak?"

I was unprepared for this. I supposed it had come from
Angelo, my well-mannered *portiere*.

"A friend," I said. "Another friend."

"I took the liberty to call the Embassy on your phone,"

he continued, "and they told me that Brenda Cloak was a student of sculpture at the American Academy."

"She left there t-ten years ago," I said loudly. "The American Embassy isn't worth shit."

"Either everybody is always everyone's friend or no one ever knows anybody," said the detective, turning to leave. Their goodbyes were cordial, or so it seemed, the one stopping to admire a Russian etching of Jerusalem that I had bought at the local flea market.

"Very valuable," he said. "You have many valuable things. It would be a shame if you ever had to leave Rome. What would you do with everything? How could you replace your own private Michelangelo?"

The other one was picking at his ear with a matchstick when they disappeared.

Benedetto would not answer his doorbell. I went around to the window but I could not see inside, and I walked back across the bridge, angry and impatient with my predicament, and immensely sad. Then I went back to work in my studio because there was nothing more I could do. Brenda was picked up by the police as she stood in front of Benedetto's house ringing the bell. I learned this later in the day when she telephoned from the police station. Benedetto's dossier was on the inspector's desk, she told me, and he tapped it ruefully with a red pencil as she answered questions.

When Brenda telephoned again it was the middle of the night. I had fallen into a deep sleep, huddled under quilts and blankets.

"He still won't answer his door," she said. "The police can't get into his house. All my things are there. They've kept me at the station all this time. I'm trying to keep calm

but it's very worrying. Can you meet me there, in Trastevere?"

I said from under the covers, "Get them to break down
the door. If Benedetto isn't there, try to get hold of his address book. They'll start pulling in all the foreigners listed
in it. It's two o'clock in the morning." I was looking now
at the clock I had knocked to the floor when I picked up
the phone. I shook it. It did not tick.

"Are you there?" asked Brenda in an anxious voice.

My anger spread through me, concentrated on the broken clock. The catastrophe of the wrecked lives, my own
auxiliary role in a tragedy I had sensed but not avoided
now found its embodiment in the pleading clock hands
stuck at ten to two.

"Give me time for a coffee," I said, and hung up.

The police were there with Brenda when I got to the
house. The streets were deserted; swaying pools of light
glowed from the overhanging lamps, intensifying the emptiness. It was so cold that there were no cats rummaging
through the alleys.

"You'll have to pay, either one of you, if we break the
door down. You'll have to pay to replace it," said one of
the policemen, the one holding the crowbar. A small knot
of people stood around the doorway, tenants of the building wearing a hastily assembled, comic assortment of
clothing. The scene was straight out of the Opera Buffa:
whispered conversation about Benedetto's noble family,
about suspicious goings-on in his apartment; eyes rolled
and there was the required critical-envious smirking and
nudging. The extra police, too, got into the act and
preened.

It was a heavy door and it took about a quarter of an
hour to wrench it from its hinges. Two policemen darted

inside with flashlights, suddenly fearful because of the intense quiet inside. The tenants crowded together and peered inside the darkened room to get a better look. Two beams met and crossed over Benedetto's body rigid at his desk.

From somewhere in space I heard the tenants metamorphose into shrieking crows, and I saw Brenda walk swiftly into the room to switch on the desk lamp and slide an address book into the sleeve of her coat. Then she rushed back and buried her head against me, the police quickly seizing a note they saw next to the pill bottle as the lamp went on. I don't remember much else about that night because I cannot trust what comes to mind. I see flashbulbs illuminating the scene: body slumped over desk, empty pill bottles, a vase with lavendar tulips. I hear the commotion in the hallways, endless footsteps up and down the stairs, several sirens. But I mistrust my memory because these seem to be movie images assembled to conceal from myself the real-life version of looking at the confirmation of my worst fears. I wondered then, as I would wonder throughout the next months, whether I would have spoken in a different way that morning had I realized that he might take his life. For, as the inspector would repeat many times that night, I was the last person to have seen him alive.

The note Benedetto left was never shown to us. But the corner of it that Brenda had been able to read said:

I cannot wait until

The newspapers did not play it up as we feared they would. Benedetto's family had good connections. His death was mentioned as heart failure due to the medicines he was taking. The apartment in Trastevere was sealed. Brenda was allowed to remove a few of her belongings wrapped in newspapers and shopping bags. Following the scare, their friends saw less of each other, and finally the self-styled Dolce Vita group dispersed and were never seen together again.

Several days after the two deaths, Angelo, the *portiere*, came to my door to tell me what a fine and honorable palazzo I inhabited and that he was displeased to find at its portals a pair of disorderly Americans who wanted to see me. I discovered, when I persuaded him to let them come upstairs, that the only disorderly thing about them was their despair, which had reduced them to monosyllables and caused them to break off phrases mid-sentence. They were the two brothers of Dennis Love who had come from Phoenix to claim his body and they had just been to the city morgue.

"The reason we're here. I mean, the reason we've come to see you . . ." began the rail-thin brother who had nervous grey eyes, "is that yours is the only name the American Embassy could give us."

I began to say that the Embassy had done me no favors in all that had happened, but thought better of it.

The other brother said simply, "We don't know why he died." He was wearing a lumber jacket and he held the passport in his hands.

I looked at them both, knowing there was nothing I could say or invent that would help, for in fact I had not known their brother very well. Maybe they understood this and had stopped by only because they were in Rome, knew nobody else, and had nothing further to do, now that they had made the arrangements to bring their brother home. I began to say that their brother had mixed pills and alcohol and in Italy they did not understand that it was a lethal combination, that we give other countries credit for information they do not have. And the reason they do not have the information is that they never needed it.

Then a strange thing happened. The thin, older brother had stood, crossed the room, restlessly touching ashtrays and refilling his drink, muttering a kind of accompaniment to what I was saying—either an endorsement or a nervous tic, I couldn't tell which, and he then left the room after asking me the way to the bathroom. I don't know why I thought it strange that he was gone so long. It could have been that recent events had made me jumpy, and my antennae were particularly sharp. But at a certain moment I heard the sound of metal falling against the tiles, then, briefly, there was the sharp odor of something burning. A short while later he returned to the living room, his quick eyes calmed, his voice slow and blurred, and he seemed to look at us from a great distance.

"Okay," he said. "I'll get through it."

The younger brother and I looked at each other mystified, and I tried again to make some conversation about Rome, including an unexpected speech about ancient civilizations diminishing the importance of our own lives. They listened obediently, poor bastards. I should have shut up and let them weep.

When, a few years ago, I described to a friend of mine, a man who runs a drug rehabilitation center, the strangeness that had come about when the brother had left the room and come back, he said that it probably had been heroin.

It was always the wild cyclamen that broke through first in the woods outside of Rome, heralding spring. The siesta hour lengthened with the warmth, the streets becoming lazy and quiet. Now that the windows were open we could hear the bells across the rooftops, the guitars from half-opened restaurant doors on the piazza, the hammering, chiseling, flower-vending, Vespa-motored, dish-clattering, aria-singing melody that is Rome's alone.

Most of us had survived the winter. Brenda disappeared after those tragic days and there was no way I could track her down, though I did not try very hard. My studio kept me busy enough and I thought I might finally make enough money to close for the summer and leave town. I had taken up with a new band of friends and on those first warm days we took picnics to the countryside, finding an abandoned church in Palombara, and next to it a flowering almond orchard. The village perched above it fit perfectly into the palm of an uplifted hand.

Walking through the center of Rome one afternoon, I took a shortcut back to my studio, passing the church of Sant'Ignazio, just near the Stock Exchange. A woman dressed in black was seated on the outside wall of the church, below a small relief of the Madonna. A slot for money had been set into the wall underneath the relief and the woman gave the impression that she hoped a charitable person might be tempted to bypass the money slot and put coins instead into her hand. She seemed, beneath her shawl, to be practicing the art of begging; that is, she put out her hand, cupped it, then turned it over as though admiring a ring. As I passed she looked up and then she quickly turned away. I think even before I saw her face I knew it was Brenda.

I moved on a few steps, then I turned, walked over to her, and said, "Get up from there, Brenda. You look ridiculous."

She said, "How can you make fun of me?"

"Making fun of you has nothing to do with what I'm

saying. I'm telling you that no one is going to give you money when there are Italian ladies acceptably poor and twice your age who could use that space."

"You're saying that because you've never had to beg."

"How do you know what I've had to do?"

"I wanted to be independent. After all, you were responsible for my teeth . . ."

"Get up, Brenda. You're making me lose my temper."

"Your eyes," she said. "They *burn* so when you're angry. They look like andirons."

And so we went to the nearest bar and had sandwiches and drinks until I remembered that I had a client due for a sitting and rushed off, asking Brenda to call me later in the day. She had told me over her prosciutto that her Dolce Vita days were over, that she had given up both men and sculpture and was considering the Church, and that she had also given up all drugs now that the really serious stuff had come to Italy, and it scared her for all those gentle Italians. (She was right. Italy easily took to drug addiction a few years later when heroin was quickly and quietly and cheaply distributed in certain areas to stir up interest. And these days, the empty syringes sparkle on the cobblestones around the Campo dei Fiore and the Piazza Navona and kids shoot up in daylight.)

She did not call that day or the next. I thought of passing Sant'Ignazio again but decided that I could not manage to play out the same scene, that this time I might start feeling sorry for her, something I did not want to do.

A few weeks later she came to the studio. By now it was full springtime and the days were sunny and warm.

"Welcome," I said. "I won't ask how you *are*, because when you are asked how you *are*, you begin with the sugar plantation in Jamaica, and then New York, Bennington, Paris . . ."

"I know what you're going to say," she said in a flat voice, placing a worn pocketbook on my desk. Then she removed a handkerchief and put it next to the pocketbook. Without warning she began to sob, dabbing at her eyes with the handkerchief, then putting it back in her pocketbook.

"I cry so much lately," she said. "I find myself preparing for it, like some kind of seizure. I cry in shops and in churches and even on the street. I cry also on park benches."

I opened my mouth, about to say something.

"I know what you're about to say," she repeated. "You're going to tell me I ought to leave Rome, leave Italy. Leave Europe."

"Yes," I said carefully. "That's just what I am going to tell you."

"But it's *spring!*" she shrieked in an anguished voice.

"It's spring there too. In fact, you would have the chance of living through two springs, if you follow me, since they're a month behind us in the States . . ."

"I don't have the money for a ticket."

"I've thought of that."

"I won't take any money from you."

"I've thought of that too. To begin with, I don't have the money to spare. But I figured out how to get it. I've got certain rich friends who've never had their pictures taken. Now, for charitable reasons, I'm going to tell them that I encountered—do you follow me?—encountered this poor woman begging at Sant'Ignazio. A poor woman, toothless . . ."

"Stop it!" cried Brenda. "I've never heard of such cruelty."

". . . who needs to go home to . . ."

". . . to Calabria," she interrupted. "To see her family one more time. Giuseppina. Her name is Giuseppina. She has twelve grandchildren, four of whom she has never seen. She came to Rome with her husband. No, she came to Rome after her husband died, to work for a family as a housekeeper . . ."

I had forgotten about Brenda's imagination.

"That's fine," I said, "that's fine. And I'm going to take their portraits, for my usual fee, for this charitable purpose. To send her home. All I need is four rich friends. Then they get their pictures and you get your ticket."

"And what do you get?"

"I get rid of you. I can't keep walking around Rome worrying that I'm going to run into you holding out a cup. Also, there's the possibility that friends of my friends will see the pictures and want their pictures taken, so it will be a kind of public relations. As long as I don't have to produce Giuseppina herself, which I doubt I'd have to do."

Brenda was quiet for a long time. I thought back to the first visit she had made to my studio. She had looked even more rumpled to me then, but I suppose I had become used to her.

"I guess I'll have to go back," she said. "I guess I can't really manage anymore."

I said, "I guess not."

"I don't know what to say. I mean, about gratitude."

"Gratitude has nothing to do with it," I said. "It's a form of self-protection. I only hope when it's my time to get out of Rome someone tells me to go."

I took four sets of photographs without trouble and no one asked me much about Giuseppina. And so Brenda Cloak left Rome, left Italy. Left Europe. On our way to the airport she kept repeating that if we just had one small accident, even a flat tire, she might miss the TWA flight and would be allowed one more day. She called out of the window to other cars, asking them to shear off my fender. We stopped for coffee on the way and she left her one pathetic piece of luggage on the seat and her door unlocked, hoping, I think, that either the car or the valise would be stolen. But we arrived at the airport on time. The countryside along the way was as beautiful as it would ever be that year, with a blur of mauve around the trees and a mist rising from the fields. The Autostrada had just been finished and I realized that I could travel up north and reach Venice within a half day. Venice . . .

I never heard from Brenda again. I knew that I wouldn't. A few years later I wrote to an address she had given me in Saratoga Springs, where she had a distant cousin. But the letter came back with this notation stamped diagonally across the envelope. It said:

HOUSE BOARDED UP

And then the postman, who had his own importance to consider, had inscribed his initials, with a flourish, underneath.

But I Meant
Edith Wharton
No Harm

It was always clear to me that my nature does not like or understand wide views, preferring always to concentrate on the courtyard rather than the hills beyond, listening carefully to the concerto but only half hearing the symphony. There are many times I consider this a disability.

When I was quite young I got into trouble with my grades at school because of my inability to grasp larger issues, like Western Civilization. Luckily I had a friend, Elliot Kaplan, who was very good at this. He was extremely bright, too bright, and was generally disliked by most of his classmates whose hands did not shoot up as quickly or as eagerly as Elliot's did when a question was asked by the teacher. Elliot never learned that this was the main reason for his unpopularity, thinking instead that it was because he wasn't good-looking or rich or athletic enough.

In return for his academic help I tried to provide a modest social life for Elliot Kaplan, dragging him along to parties and dances, wherever I was invited, and, looking back, I seem to have been invited out a good deal. As the days and years flashed by, Elliot, an extravagant reader, began to wear glasses, the same year that he finally got rid of the

braces masking his teeth, so he effectively exchanged one
metallic impediment for another. I seem to have slid effortlessly past this awkward era with neither braces nor
glasses, and by the time I was seventeen my vanity had
reached truly monumental proportions.

We left for colleges at different coasts, writing frequent
letters full of earnest philosophical discoveries and other
more pressing matters, most of them having to do with our
sexual exploits. Elliot was drawn to shaggy-haired girls
who painted bad pictures, though invariably they compen-
sated for failing his high artistic standards by providing a
peppy sexual abandon not indicated by their modest,
mousy manners. However, in his wide scheme of things
(Elliot's horizons, unlike mine, were always wide) these
companions had no place, for they would never gain him
the social and professional position he sought.

We kept our friendship intact even though it seemed to
me that Elliot had turned into a relentless intellectual, too
concerned with the civilized refinements of the elite. And
Elliot's view of me, he said, varied between my being a
hedonist, and a hedonist manqué.

I was unexpectedly invited on a boat trip cruising along
the coast of North Africa the summer of my seventeenth
birthday, the same summer that I heard from Elliot about a
meeting in Tangier. He had been awarded a scholarship at
the Sorbonne, and because he had managed to save some
money working part-time as a waiter, he was taking a
month's vacation with a new girlfriend, traveling through
Spain and across the Strait of Gibraltar. It seemed a fine
idea to meet in such an exotic place, so we made the date
by mail, for late August.

The phrase *Beautiful People* was not yet in use. But

even though we lacked this classification, the group collected for the yacht, called the *Wicked Witch,* was
weighted down with enough combined narcissism to sink
us as soon as we got on board. The boat was owned by a
school friend's father, a man from Los Angeles prominent
in the film business. He also sent an older daughter to ac-
company us as chaperone and keep us chaste, a gesture any
fool could have foretold was doomed. All told, there was a
baker's yeasty dozen aboard, including the eager crew.
Among other things, I was expected to play the piano—
which I did quite well in those days—a small upright
manacled to the wall. I diligently played it our first night
out, Scriabin, I think it was, and never again. I decided,
just like everyone else, to settle down to the business of
frivolous enjoyment.

And so we were quite a carefree group when we an-
chored off the coast of Tangier, aggressively suntanned,
somewhat androgynous, wearing our smallest of bathing
suits—the bikini had recently come into style—on our
quick-sketch, unfinished bodies, our short hair somewhat
fairer than it had been two weeks before when we had assembled at Idlewild Airport for the fifteen-hour air trip to
Casablanca. The film maker's daughter, Elaine, had gathered us together from both coasts and we tried to make
her proud of her choices.

Although, as I say, our friendship was reciprocal, there
was also an edge of competition between Elliot and me. I
certainly had it in mind to display my gilded boatmates to
him, each one with immensely successful fathers and eter-
nally slim mothers, all lately on the lookout for acceptable
sons-in-law. These enticements were, I imagined, a far cry
from the opportunities offered Elliot by the High School

of Music and Art graduate he would surely have in tow
and complain about.

Tangier, then, was a free port. Money was sold on the
streets; vendors carried blackboards chalked in with the
latest exchange rates, and all up and down the street leading to the Casbah, the shouted quotations competed with
the other, more sensual sounds of the chanting muezzin,
the oud, the snake charmers, rug sellers, brass merchants,
and many-tongued tourists. I spotted Elliot at a café on the
upstairs terrace of the Hotel Fuentes, a seedy place on the
Socco Chico that I believe still stands. We waved to each
other energetically, and I rushed upstairs to find him opposite a girl so unlike my earlier image that I thought, somehow, that he had made a mistake and was seated at the
wrong table.

She was very pale and blond, her hair cut short and
curved under in a pageboy style. She looked like the hero-
ine of a British novel from the twenties, prim, beautifully
bred, modest, and very sensible, with the possibility of an
unruly fire beneath her calm exterior. When she began to
talk I realized that she was as bright as Elliot and within an
hour I understood, with a wretched lurch in my heart, that
they were in love. Unassisted by my connivance, Elliot
had found exactly what he wanted.

Her name was Sally James, from Virginia, where her
family had for generations dwelt in ease and comfort
among rolling hills, with horses and tobacco in abundance.
They held hands as the sun lowered behind the tower of
the nearby mosque, and I saw that I was now entering a
new phase with Elliot Kaplan, a phase marked for the first
time by envy. Deep into my E. M. Forster period, Sally
James was just the girl I had secretly imagined for myself.
When I left them and returned to the boat, I found my

eyes slitting down as I studied all my spoiled fellow travelers sprawled half naked on the decks pretending to read
Paris-Match and drinking Pernods. I looked back at the
shore and I said to the torpid air, overcome by the ro-
mance of the Moroccan harbor and the memory of the
pale girl seated at the café table, "Sally. Oh, Sally. Surely
you would prefer me to Elliot." But the warm African
breezes carried my words quite sensibly out to sea.

The next day my boat friends went on a tour to Tetuán
and I met with Elliot and Sally on the ramparts of the city,
high above the Mediterranean. In the distance we could see
the *Wicked Witch,* luxurious and somewhat larger than
the other boats. I sat, as usual, with my back to the view.
My expression was grim. I tried to keep myself from seeking stolen glances at Sally. But it was not just Sally. Both
of them, by their seriousness, seemed to reproach me for
the triviality implied by my way of life. They were so
knowledgeable about everything, so thorough! They had
just come from Seville buoyed up by the complete history,
it seemed, of Spain. Now in Morocco, Elliot allowed himself a monologue on how Tangier was received by En-
gland as a dowry when Catherine of Braganza married
Charles II. It was very interesting, of course—Elliot was
usually interesting—but their intellectual earnestness was
frankly tedious, and they had already begun to finish sentences for each other.

"You know," said Elliot, "the Moslems got as far as the
Pyrenees in the eighth century." He crossed his legs and
tilted back in his chair. "They took Narbonne and Car-
cassonne."

"And Nîmes," put in Sally, tapping Elliot lightly on his
shoulder. She was wearing a flowered sleeveless dress,
which, I thought moodily, would be called a frock. A

flowered frock. Oh, Forster! Oh, seventeen! "Imagine France as a Moslem country," she added.

I tried to imagine it and failed. I had never been to France. I took out a long reed pipe I had been given by a Moroccan sailor and filled its small clay bowl with kif. Inhaling with pleasure, I sat back in my chair as the waiter approached us, his babouches slapping against the tile of the terrace. He set down small glasses filled with mint leaves; then from high above the table he poured the tea out of a blue enameled pot. The tea glistened and bubbled in the sunlight.

"I'd thought maybe you'd come on board," I said, realizing even as I said it that my boastful plan to show off my chums would fall on deaf ears.

"You're kind to ask," said Sally. "But there's so much to see. We're leaving for Fez tomorrow. We thought of trying to follow the path of Edith Wharton."

"It was Wharton's visit here with General Lyautey that gave us the idea to come to Morocco," remarked Elliot over his shoulder.

I did not know who this general was, and as this information was deeply uninteresting to me, I wondered how I could get back to the boat as fast as possible to continue my smoking privately under the benign skies of the Mediterranean.

Sally said in a pink voice, "Do you always sit with your back to the view?" Elliot said blankly, yes, he invariably does, and I answered that if the three of us were ever going to get along, we had better start immediately by being less condescending, mainly to me, and to leave out any further talk of Catherine of Braganza or Edith Wharton, or any other such lofty items, and concentrate on the Moorish arch just behind us where an elderly Arab with the opaque eyes of blindness was nonetheless managing to filch a package of cigarettes from a nearby tabletop.

This speech, the clarity of which was magnified in my mind by the kif I was smoking, was suddenly interrupted by Sally, her eyes fixed on the vastness of the sea below us. She pushed her chair back and ran to the railing of the terrace.

"Someone's fallen from a boat," she cried.

Elliot and I rushed over to her at the edge of the terrace. Way below us a small speedboat had just come to an abrupt stop and its driver was waving his hands. Behind the boat, on a long line, dragged an empty pair of water skis. Another man at the stern dove into the water, surfaced, and circled the area around the skis.

None of us said anything. Other people on the terrace, realizing that something was happening in the midst of that picturesque view, crowded against the railing to watch. Again and again the man went under the water, searched, returned to the surface. The driver finally managed to signal to another boat and it came over at top speed, rocking in its wake all the other boats moored there. Soon there were five or six boats around the same small place on the surface of the sea.

The agitation I felt with my friends now had found its tangible form. I looked down at the water, at that small watery space—or absence of space—where everything was focused; then I turned my back and studied each detail of the terrace, the slant of the sun on the tables, the facial expressions of the waiters, anything not to turn back to the wide view.

I heard Sally's voice cry out and I turned to see the driver surface, holding a limp form. Someone else jumped into the water from another boat, and they both pulled the glistening body up over the motorboat and onto its deck. We saw this from so far away that it had the quality of a tiny mechanical spectacle. The people on our terrace finally found their voices, walked back to their tables, brought their drinks to the railing. Soon the inert figure began to move. We could hear a muffled cheer rise from the boats below, and on the terrace we, too, cheered.

The three of us hugged each other, exhilarated, united by this triumph of life that was not of our doing. Now, filled with universal reflections (for our perch way above the water gave us something of a Creator's view), we looked at each other with more charity. The remainder of the day was spent roaming through the souks. In the evening we danced on the patio of the El Minzah, the lights of Spain way in the distance. In good spirits, I left them late at night. But when I walked back to the marina I let myself feel a sharp pain I had avoided, would always try to avoid, and I can only explain that it was as though I had been grasped unwillingly by the shadowy hands of other people's happiness.

The *Wicked Witch* sailed the next day to Mogador, and so I did not see Elliot Kaplan and Sally James again in Morocco. By the time our group was winding its way in a convoy of hired jeeps from Mogador to Marrakesh, I'd given up the idea of winning Sally away from Elliot, my devouring adolescent raptures now concentrating on what waited behind those pale rose crenellated walls up ahead on the horizon.

Elliot managed to stretch his scholarship to last two years at the Sorbonne and we wrote to each other occasionally. I learned that Sally's family had managed to separate them, and for a long while he didn't mention her at all. Back in New York he became an assistant professor at

Barnard, keeping company again with those dark girls with furrowed brows and artistic sensibilities. Then one day he disappeared. It was unusual for an assistant professor to disappear before the spring semester was over and there was a flurry of concern among the members of the faculty. I suspected that he'd gone back to Europe and was not surprised when he reappeared several months later in Paris married to Sally James.

It was not until six or seven years later that I saw them both in their apartment in Paris on the rue St.-Louis-en-l'Île, a few years after the birth of their son Kenneth. Elliot had recently become involved with the *Paris Review*, and although he worked as a free-lance editor, his real ambition was to publish his own stories. Their splendid apartment was subleased from an art dealer who had moved to Buenos Aires for five years, and Sally had brought over her family silver, a few paintings and bound books. Sally had grown even thinner and now wore her hair in a severe fashion, pulled back to form a chignon. Elliot's face had caught up with his features and now his hairline was receding.

The child, of course, was uniquely bright, and unexpectedly merry, given the relentless seriousness of his parents. Nonetheless, I was still very fond of them and I admired their precocious minds. I heard myself say that I was no longer the hedonist of earlier days, and I immediately regretted it because it sounded like an apology for the past.

If Elliot mentioned too many current literary names in the course of our conversation, I decided not to let it bother me. I was pleased that he seemed to know every writer in Paris and that the Kaplans could afford to entertain them in style. In addition to discovering every corner of Paris, memorizing its history and quoting its literature, Elliot had become an authority on food and wine, and Sally went to the Bibliothèque Nationale every afternoon to collect material for a biography of the Marquise de Maintenon that she thought she might one day write, though, as she often repeated, it was understood that Elliot was the writer in the family.

When a brief space occurred during their monologues, it was with considerable enthusiasm and at some length that I managed to tell them I was on my way to find locations for a film I would be making in the Auvergne, a region known for its bad weather, its uninviting landscape, and its obstinate, dour resistance to change.

Once the film was finished I decided to edit it in Nice because it would be cheaper than in the States. Since it was out of season, I easily found a furnished place a block above the Boulevard des Anglais, and I remember almost nothing about the apartment except that everything was prudently covered in plastic. Also, I recall that after I left for the film studio each day, the concierge reliably entered the apartment in hope of finding damage or thievery or, better still, signs of immorality. I spoke every now and then with the Kaplans, whose existence up north in Paris had become a symbol of civilized living to me. They promised to visit, and, surprising me, they did come, in mid-February.

They took rooms at the Carlton in Cannes. We sat under the wide awning of the terrace watching the season's first fashionable tourists parade along the Croisette, probably the most successful showing-off promenade in Europe. The day was unseasonably hot, and on the boulevard cruising motorists seductively restrained their powerful sports cars. Far on the horizon there was a sailboat

race, and every now and then Sally would reach languidly
for her binoculars to watch them, her dark glasses perched
on top of her head. Elliot talked about where we would
have dinner, a certain restaurant he had remembered somewhere in the hills, their specialty of *loup de mer*, and the
particular *vin de Provence* they served that he always had
trouble finding in Paris. Kenneth, by now nine—his mirth-
ful expression had survived—slowly ate his lemon sherbet,
saving the *gaufrette* wafer until the very end. If I have
made the Kaplans sound too overrefined, too self-indul-
gent, I regret it, for although these qualities might have
particularized them, they were graceful about requiring
the best, using the same diligence to acquire the vast
amount of culture they always had at the ready. I guessed
Elliot was still raising his hand as he had done so long ago
at school.

I picked up the binoculars to scan the horizon, remembered our time in Tangier, and wondered why we always
seemed to be scanning such wide panoramas that were not
to my liking.

"It's remarkable," I began, about to refer to these coin-
cidences.

"Yes, but it's even better from our balcony upstairs,"
said Elliot, crediting, instead, the view.

One day during their visit I saw them by chance in the
marketplace at Antibes buying picnic things for an outing.
Before going over to them I watched for a while as they
chose the pâté, the watercress, the berries. Kenneth had
wandered off to gaze at a performing mime. And, unexpectedly, I let myself feel the full force of my longing for
their ordered lives, another fine example of how we de-
ceive ourselves about the people we think we know. Un-

willing to dwell on this, I went over to them, and immediately we were filled with smiles and picnic plans.

It was then that they told me they had been talking it over and decided that maybe it would be a good idea, if I agreed, to leave Kenneth with me for a few days. We seemed to get along so well and have such fun together, they said. It was out of character for them to act impulsively, and I was delighted with the idea. Sally added that Kenneth was getting too insulated being with them all the time, that he ought to see a more bohemian side of life. I took it well, though I thought the word *bohemian* had gone out in the thirties.

It was a good piece of luck for me. I was going through one of my anti-French phases, irritated by so many sulky, unresponsive Niçoise neighbors in a part of the Mediterranean that had until this century remained attached to amiable Italy. I understood then that national and temperamental boundaries are as clear as map makers make them out to be, changing dyes at the border (pink Italy to blue France).

The second day he was with me I took Kenneth to the caves at St.-Cézaire. We arrived there just as the grottos were closing, and so we rushed through the many-hued Hall of Draperies, the Organ Chamber, and the Great Hall, hurried along by an impatient guide who managed, just before we left, to knock out the first bars of *La Marseillaise* on the low-hanging stalactites. Kenneth was very happy with this. When we left it had begun to rain, the sky suddenly swept with black clouds.

St.-Cézaire is high above Grasse in the hills of the Maritime Alps. The road curves through the gorges of the Loup River, and the views, for those who like them, are spectacular. But when there is a hard rain, the rivers of

Provence swell, and I remembered, while driving, the sudden storm that broke the dam in nearby Fréjus and drowned several thousand people only about six years before.

The storm, that February afternoon, came out of nowhere with a tropical intensity. The small car I then owned was built too close to the ground, more of a boat than a car, sending waves of water spraying the curbs. Its history was bad; it had absorbed gasoline like a sponge, its horn, its cooling system, its clutch, its carburetor, and its windshield wipers had given out at various points during my stay in Nice. In this fierce rainfall, with the waters rushing through the roads, rushing, it would seem, like everything else along the coast, to the sea, there was no reason not to expect the worst.

I kept trying to find level ground. Now I was on the back roads near no town. The sky was evenly black, and through the smudged windshield I saw the occasional lights of other cars coming toward me. The sound of the rain and the rushing water was like the sound of a storm in the mid-Atlantic. Over it, I spoke reassuringly to Kenneth, who sat with an apprehensive look beside me.

"My feeling," said Kenneth, trying to smile, "is that we're going to be stuck here for a few days. And my momma, as you call her, and my poppa, are going to be very surprised when I don't turn up in Paris." Then he laughed. "What fun," he said, though I could not tell whether he meant it.

As though waiting for Kenneth's validation, the car stopped. There was no coaxing it; the motor would not turn over and the road was filled with an onrushing river of water. I saw all the rest of it in my mind. I sighed. It is a bad habit of mine, sighing when I see bleakness ahead.

Hearing me sigh, Kenneth sighed. And so we sat in the car sighing as the waters rose. Naturally I had no umbrella. After taking off my shoes and socks and rolling up my trousers, I got out of the car and tried to hail a passing car. The few drivers who went by were too busy navigating what had become a sudden river, too worried for themselves. I began to see it as a foreigner's parable.

Outside the car I was drenched in an instant; slogging forward, I pushed the car over to the edge of the road halfway onto a field. Reassuring Kenneth that I would be right back, I went in search of a house.

But the houses were all closed, ghost dwellings on a ghostly, billowing night. When I came to a large iron gate the sign read SANATORIUM, putting the idea of madness into my head, but it, too, was locked with a chain. I kept returning to the car to see whether Kenneth was all right, and each time I found him trying to find it funny. But after a while we both understood that the rain was not going to stop and that it was not funny. For long periods we sat in the car shivering with the cold and damp. Then I would explore another side road, wading above my knees in the rising water. The storm, in the darkness, was a maniac's howling. I understood for the first time how people and animals, trees, cars and houses, could be uprooted and carried swiftly away. Finally I found a lighted house and rang its bell. From behind the shuttered window upstairs came a hoarse, tentative "Yes? Who is it?"

I said, "I'm in trouble. I don't know where I am. My car has stalled." I would have continued shouting my grievances to the shuttered light above but I was interrupted.

"And what do you want, monsieur?"—the formality of the question silencing me, as if a silence could have been noted in that streaming downpour.

"A telephone. A taxi," I cried, the water running into my eyes and mouth.

"Ah, *non*, monsieur. There are no taxis . . ."

I lost control. I do not know what I then shouted to that window. A spasm of frenzy shook me. All my loathing for provincial France, for being forever a stranger on some alien doorway, combined into a dizzying malediction that left me feeling something close to euphoria, still trying to keep my balance in the swirling floodwaters as I watched the unblinking light above.

Lurching back to the car, I found Kenneth next to it trying in the torrent to flag down some help. When I forced him back inside the useless car his teeth were chattering, and I saw that now we were in real danger. I got a picnic blanket out of the trunk, wrapped him in it, and at that moment a flashlight scanned our car. A truck built well above the ground had appeared out of nowhere and a man got out holding an umbrella.

"I asked you to wait a minute," he muttered. "I was upstairs watching television," he added without charm. "You were yelling so loud you couldn't hear me. Get your son inside the truck and I'll drive you both to a railroad station."

We obliged, driving in near-silence through the crashing sea to La Napoule on the coast. Kenneth came down with the flu and the incident quickly caused a rent in the fabric of the Kaplans' lives that—like all such pivotal accidents— would reveal its deterioration. Once he was back in Paris, Kenneth's condition never really cleared up, and not unexpectedly, Sally decided to take him to a specialist in the States. After a few uneasy months, he was cured, and by then Sally wanted to stay in Virginia. Even though his buddies at the *Paris Review* had packed up and returned to

New York, acknowledging that neither France nor anywhere else was the center of literary life, it was difficult
for Elliot to leave Paris. An era had passed, as it always
does, without anyone much taking notice. Now his study
looked out on an English garden in need of care.

So much for my bohemian life.

By then I was living in Rome. When I came to America
for a vacation I visited them. I had always suspected a re-
sidual anger toward me, if not for the incident of the
flood, then surely for the unexpected turn of events that
brought them home. But they had never blamed me for it,
even at the time when they flew from Paris, seized Kenneth from my guest room, and planted him in a hospital.
Now, in Virginia, I found Kenneth brimming with fine
health and amusing stories, and I was relieved to hear him
talk of our time in Nice with such pleasure. But the household was oppressive, and both Elliot and Sally spent too
much time worrying over meals and the quality of the
larkspur and the hollyhocks. As though confirming this
pervasive unease, the creek outside their house was coated
with thousands of bloated fish, poisoned by the industrial
wastes of the Potomac River upstream. The word *pollu-
tion* and its tandem word *ecology* had just begun to appear
in the newspapers, and we sailed joylessly through the
crust of dead fish, playing difficult word games and making plans to join a peace march in Washington.

I was anxious to get back to Europe. I suppose I had
begun to see America as a foreigner would, for by now I
felt myself a foreigner wherever I was, which is one of the
penalties and illusions of living abroad.

"You keep talking about Rome with such sentiment,"
Sally remarked. "Like something out of Henry James or
Edith Wharton."

"Edith Wharton again," I said, having a weirdly selective memory, particularly for details a dozen years old. Sally looked over at me bewildered.

We were walking together alone in the fields behind the wide Tudor house. I noted that Sally's features had become sharper—almost bird-like—one of the destinies of those English-heroine faces.

"I should never have married a Jew," she said suddenly. "Oh, don't look at me with your eyebrows raised. It's not for the reasons you might think I mean. It's because there is no way Elliot can understand the continuity I feel with the land, the country. My family has been in Virginia since 1640. Sixteen-forty! That's what? Ten or eleven generations?" She stopped mid-step and sat abruptly on the grass, running her hands across it with affection. "The land, everything here has been ours for so long. We're all buried in the same cemetery and some of the stones look like ancient artifacts. But they're all *us!*"

I spread out my arms in a mock gesture of embracing a dozen generations of landed Virginians.

"Yes," she said in a loud voice. "We belong! Or at least I do. Elliot doesn't have this—how can I say it?—this personal *geology*. His grandparents came to New York only sixty years ago without a word of English. And New York isn't even really America. He can't, well, *connect* anywhere." She looked at me now with a face pale and sorrowing.

I ventured, "He was happy in Paris . . ."

"But I was not. Not really. I want to stay put! My father has loaned us this big house. There are a lot of books, and there's the bay just behind the property. We could have a sailboat . . ." Her voice was full of tears. "I don't need to keep moving, keep acquiring other places. *I've al-*

ways known who I am. That's what I mean about Elliot . . ."

Her mind went toiling on, and I realized that she would nurse her grievances, breathing sparks onto them until they flamed high.

"I wish you would stop mentioning the virtues of Rome," she added, looking away, "you might find him on your doorstep."

When I left I went to New York, taking a ship back to Italy. As the ship—the *Cristoforo Colombo,* I think it was—eased out of the dock toward Naples, I gave a sigh of relief. The Kaplans' troubles, the whole country's troubles were not mine. Italy's secret then was that its foreigners could live there undisturbed and protected, and I was anxious to get back to Rome to wander through its familiar streets and squares, like hallways and rooms in my own home, its strollers actors in my own play. If this was an escapist's view, it didn't matter. I was returning to it and I was grateful.

I sat in the lounge as the ship edged along the margins of Manhattan, looking across the room to see who I might get in trouble with. I knew that the rule on a ship's crossing was that the genuinely interesting passengers only come out on deck the last night on board. But by nature impatient, I got up and wandered through the corridors, returning again to the lounge. The Statue of Liberty had receded into the distance, transformed now into a slim reed rising from a stagnant pond. The lounge was vast, filled with the "Italian Modern" furniture of the period, designed during the so-called economic miracle that had recently restored the pride and the treasury of postwar Italy. In the brilliant afternoon sunlight slanting through the wide porthole I tried to distinguish a misty figure dwarfed by the large leather and chrome chair upon which she sat. Her pale blond hair was pulled back—rolled back—from her forehead and temple to reveal a patrician profile as crisp as the Queen of Diamonds in a deck of playing cards. The sun was in my eyes, and, squinting, I saw that she was sipping tea—the cup, in the strong light, was translucent—and to further haze the unclear image, a screen of smoke rose from the ashtray next to her.

How people behave when they are alone in public places has always interested me, and I have frequently become drawn to attractive individuals only because of the way they stand looking out to sea, or sit reading in the sun, or behave in any of the other postures of solitude, postures in which their aloneness infers no apology. In one elliptical motion she set down her teacup, brought her hand to a watch that hung on a gold chain around her neck, consulted the time, let the watch fall against her beige jersey, and stood. Her eyes did not search the room; she did not hesitate about her direction. She simply walked out of the room. I could not have imagined that the same spherical watch of deep blue cloisonné would rest one day inside a small box in my bureau drawer. I seldom look at it and it has not kept time for a long while. But it pleases me to know that it is there. I do not think that she misses it, and I have never understood how—or whether—she had been able to read the microscopic numbers on its dime-sized gold face.

She did not appear again at dinner or for lunch the next day. I began to think that I had invented her, a figure rising in dancing motes of smoke-filled sunlight to sail coolly out of the main salon. But late in the second afternoon I was walking on the topmost deck past the kennel and found her holding aloft a small dachshund, its ears flying in the breeze.

"Don't let him fly away," I said against the wind.

"What?" she asked, strands of her imperial coiffure blowing this way and that.

"Don't let him fly away," I shouted, sounding more foolish the second time.

"Ah, I don't think there is any fear of that."

Her voice, too, was elegant. She smiled the way dog owners smile when a passerby admires their animal, looking not at me but at her treasured dachshund. I smiled, in turn, at the faraway horizon, continuing on around the deck, the wind roaring in my ears.

My memory is now hazy about the rest of that trip. I cannot remember, for example, when or why we had our first real conversation, or when we decided to change tables in the dining room in order to be able to sit with each other, or which night we became lovers. But I have a ship's photograph solidly freezing one isolated frame of the voyage. The two of us are seated in the nightclub and in front of us is an unused party hat of metallic paper. The picture, which must have been taken at the ship's gala, disturbs me, because I am looking at her with too much admiration, leaning too close to hear what she is saying. She is seated upright, perfectly poised, with the same expression on her face that she had that first day, smiling into the middle distance.

Her name, Madeleine, suited her, its languid sound as mutable as the sea. She rarely talked about herself and was particularly adept at turning the conversation around to avoid personal questions. But because she felt protected or screened by the noise and general merriment of the gala that evening, I learned a few facts that seemed romantic at the time, and perhaps they were. It was a history filled with good breeding and fancy educational institutions, a marriage to a soldier and an early divorce after the birth of a child. Her daughter, who would have been somewhat younger than myself, had grown up in many distinguished locations, but Madeleine drifted slowly, inevitably to Rome. Even during our most passionate moments, we found ourselves speaking, inexplicably, in French or Italian, as though by this verbal dislocation we could create a place-free atmosphere (enhanced by the ship itself) in which she would feel protected. The sharp details of her life ultimately wavered in fluid patterns which she accentuated by certain eccentric remarks:

"My dream is to live in a hotel room," she said that evening while the band applied itself to a bright medley of Neapolitan favorites.

"Not in Rome," she added, where it seemed she lived in a fine terrace apartment, "but in an obscure city like Aleppo, with no possessions, no passport."

"I don't know Aleppo," I said.

"Neither do I," she said, lighting a Gauloise. "Oh, I wouldn't want it to be a place I know! Just"—she paused— "just a place that is undefined. That is the whole point."

Concentrating elsewhere, she shook the match in a slow arc. I thought it would burn her fingers.

"Yes, Aleppo would be fine," she repeated, "or, I don't know, Biloxi, Mississippi." She smiled. Her mouth and her eyes were surrounded by lightly etched lines that in years to come would be a network of distinguished paths. Her eyes, the palest of turquoise, looked past me, and it was then that the ship's photographer raised his camera.

She disembarked in Naples surrounded by a mass of matched luggage, her dachshund, and a cage of finches.

Because it was Italy and still summertime, and she was so unusually beautiful, she swept past the admiring customs officials in a blur of blue eyes and aristocratic manners. She was met by a pretty girl wearing a maid's uniform, whom she introduced as Giglia. Then, while I went to look for my suitcases, they got into the back seat of a black car and disappeared into the chaos of Naples.

I had been back in Rome only a few weeks when Elliot telephoned from the airport at Fiumicino. I realized that I was more irritated than pleased. I had certain possessive feelings about Rome. He'd had his Paris, his country house in Virginia, his marriage and his child. He could have left me my Rome.

He said on the phone, "The letters S.P.Q.R., I discovered, mean Senatus Populusque Romanus, and since I've already seen it imprinted on the sides of taxis, I guess I find myself in Rome. Remember the days at school we used to look after each other? Well, I've left Sally and I've decided to try it on my own. It's your fault that I came to Rome. You spoke about it with such feeling. Now you can help me find a place to live. I expect to stay a long time."

So that was it: back again into our old roles. I nodded at the phone like an old sea captain, squinting at it through the smoke from the cigarette clenched between my teeth.

I said, "Welcome."

It was late August. The tradition was that everyone who had a little bit of money saved or a relative living in the country left Rome and went elsewhere. A vapor of heat cloaked the streets and squares. Stray cats sunned themselves on unused steps by day or lurked at night in vacant alleys and unvisited ruins. Elliot had chosen an empty time to confront Rome. But I'd heard of a vacant apartment abutting the Teatro Marcello and the various columns and fallen capitals surrounding it, though its dark living room faced a dank, airless courtyard. Elliot looked at it and signed the lease immediately, occupying Rome without a ripple.

There was no Roman equivalent of the *Paris Review,* there were no bibliophiles; Rome offered none of the cerebral intensity of the serious European capitals. I wondered how Elliot would manage. But within six months he knew the whereabouts of such details as the fifth-century encaustic painting of the Virgin and Child (in the church of Santa Francesca Romana) and he dragged me to the Protestant Cemetery to show me the exact place where Trelawny buried Shelley's ashes, having seized the poet's heart from his funeral pyre.

The oppressive heat of August had passed, and I reopened my studio and went back to work. The streets were once again filled with Romans, and old rhythms resumed. I saw Madeleine at a concert given at the Gonfalone, a small deconsecrated oratorio just off the Via Giulia. She was seated next to a young woman so similar to her in appearance that she could only have been her daughter, Jenny, who lived in Rhodes. They sat in the high-backed choir stalls in the chancel, impressively following the music, and neither of them stirred. When they applauded, only their hands seemed to move.

After the concert I was introduced to Jenny and received a pleasant, remote smile. In those days I was easily jostled into speech by someone else's sluggish silence, and I talked too much, realized it, and quickly said goodbye. Her after-image stayed with me for a few days, and I half expected to run into her on the Via Condotti or the Piazza del Popolo, where everyone congregated at the end of the day. But then Madeleine invited me to lunch and asked me to bring a friend, "a contemporary of yours," she said, "not mine." I reached for the phone, as in the dim past, and called Elliot. Elliot could do the talking this time.

The lunch was at Romolo, a restaurant in Trastevere where, Elliot explained, Raphael's mistress was supposed to have lived. The sunlit garden out in back was shielded by an aged grapevine that Elliot assured us predated Garibaldi. Jenny was less remote than at the concert. I was again surprised by the similarity-difference between the mother and daughter. Because of the inevitable comparison, Madeleine seemed even more diffuse and Jenny appeared in sharper relief than either of them really were. Jenny's unruly hair fell across her shoulders, and when she talked, she tossed her head, the air around her shattering into fragments of light. In a voice delicately shaded with a mid-Atlantic accent, she said that she could no longer stay in Rhodes while everything revolutionary was happening elsewhere.

"Jenny cares so much about these things," said Madeleine to Elliot and me. "I'm always surprised that she is my daughter."

I could not keep myself from remarking, "I'll bet you're going to say that none of it makes any difference."

"Well, it doesn't. Not to me," said Madeleine.

I opened my mouth to say something when Jenny put her hand over mine.

"Don't," she said.

I kept her hand there with my fingers and she smiled and picked up the menu with her free hand. The dappled light stretched across the starched tablecloth indiscriminately touching surfaces and enhancing them, spread-

ing across the garden, shifting with the light breeze of
early autumn.

Madeleine was a fine hostess. Because she did not take
herself seriously, she managed to enforce her light-
heartedness on those around her, and before long we began
to laugh. Even Elliot yielded to the laughter as it quickly
became one of those Roman lunches, full of anecdote and
merriment. The waiter took our order with an amiable
formality while a guitarist sang to a nearby table (where
they chatted discreetly in low voices, while ours rose with
mirth). The wine carafes were thinly covered with frost;
the sky, seen through the shifting vine leaves, was . . .

But these are the ramblings of someone struck with an
unbearable nostalgia. I have understood the need to retain
a balanced memory for the purposes of this narrative, but
here it is a losing game. Those faultless times in the
dappled light with the crisp cloths and the good company,
surrounded by the benevolent earth of Italy, were the best
times there for all of us.

It did not seem significant that when we left that lunch
the calm was punctuated by sirens, or that a troop of
armed police had formed near the Campo dei Fiori to
break up an unscheduled march of a then obscure Leftist
organization. Instead we remarked on the bursting flower
stalls and the political slogans now defacing the statue of
Giordano Bruno, burned just there for heresy in 1600. We
barely noticed the leaflets that fell like giant confetti from
the brilliant sky advising the Romans of the meeting of a
newly formed neo-Fascist party, or the petition, at the
table in the corner of the square, to legalize divorce. In the
aftermath of the parade the caffès filled up once again with
clients tilting back in their chairs to get the last good out

of the warming sun, newspapers unread in their laps, telling them that in France the students were preparing a revolution.

We walked back to Madeleine's apartment for coffee, pausing at the Piazza Navona. Our eyes dwelt, in quick succession, upon the vastness of Domitian's arena, upon Bernini's central Fountain of the Rivers, and upon a legless man propped up on its marble rim—beneath the monumentally draped, hidden gaze of the Nile—carefully combing and recombing his raven hair in the water's spray. When we arrived at the apartment we surprised Madeleine's housekeeper, who was cleaning the floor by skating across the ceramic tiles with cloths underneath her slippers. The radio was playing *Il Cielo nell'una Stanza*, and the girl, Giglia, was singing at the top of her voice.

"Skating and singing," said Madeleine. "Now, that is *my* Italy."

Embarrassed, Giglia quickly disappeared into the kitchen. When she brought the coffee out to the terrace, her cheeks were still attractively flushed.

"Giglia," said Madeleine kindly, "I want you to show these two gentlemen the view from the *altana*. I think I've drunk too much to make it up that miserable iron staircase. I'm feeling a bit rickety myself."

Jenny came with us and we looked briefly at the jumble of rooftops leading to the pine-covered hills of the villa Borghese.

Giglia said, "When I have time off, I paint. I come up here and keep painting this view. Over and over."

"And they're good," said Jenny. In this light her eyes had turned a deep blue. "If you like panoramas," and here she paused, smiling, watching a nearby rooftop where a woman of ample proportions reclaimed her laundry from a clothesline.

Elliot said, politely, "Can we see them?"

Giglia turned away. She was a lively girl with a plain face surrounded by a mass of shaggy hair. I noticed as we had climbed the short spiral staircase to the loggia that she had very pretty, unshaven legs.

"No," she said, after reflection.

"The coffee is getting cold," called Madeleine from below. "And I thought you didn't like views," she added, I thought, to me.

"I certainly don't," said Jenny emphatically, answering her. Then she added, in a softer voice, running her fingers lightly across the petal of an oleander, "It's the details that I prefer . . . I like views mainly when I can turn my back on them."

I swung Jenny around, surprising her. "You don't have to explain that to me," I said.

Later, while Jenny was showing Elliot through the vast apartment, I sat with Madeleine on the terrace. Through some acoustical trick, Viennese waltzes, played on a phonograph in a nearby palazzo, floated toward us as though the musicians were assembled in the living room. With the buildings now almost silhouettes in the last of the autumn light, I felt the same dislocation in time I had always experienced when I was alone with Madeleine.

Madeleine said, "I don't go out very much. I don't see very many people. I prefer to be alone. You must have understood that when we met on the ship. Because it was a ship, we were able to become very close, very quickly." She paused to light a cigarette, and it was evident that what she was saying was difficult for her. "It was right—if you see what I mean—for then. Now that particular closeness is over, even though, of course, we will be friends, I hope, for a long, long time. What I'm really trying to say is that I saw"—coughing, she waved away the smoke—"or, rather, I understood what passed between you and Jenny. You're alike, you know, in many ways."

I found myself visited by conflicting feelings of elation and remorse, both of them exhilarating.

"I speak so infrequently of personal things," she said. "What I'm trying to tell you is that I understand what is taking place between you and it makes me extremely happy."

Madeleine kept her eyes on the rooftops a long time. Then she smiled and touched me lightly on the face. We turned to the darkening waltz-filled rooms behind us as the laughter of Elliot and Jenny sounded along the corridor. It was then that Madeleine managed to remove from her neck the blue cloisonné watch she had worn on the ship going to Naples and, in a continuing gesture, placed it in my hand, her own hand moving on to her lips where an index finger, poised vertically, formed the dual gesture of a blown kiss and a vow of shared secrecy.

When Elliot walked me to my studio, both of us were drunk, euphoric, listing dangerously toward the cobblestones.

He said loudly, "She was *wonderful!* My God, she was *really* wonderful!" It was an unlikely utterance from him.

I said warily, "Which one, the mother or the daughter."

He looked briefly puzzled. "Giglia!" he cried, enraptured. "Giglia, the maid who paints panoramas on her lunch hour." And with that, he lurched on his way.

Elliot's courtship of Giglia was impressive, a still-married man from New York trying to persuade a provin-

cial girl from Busto Arsizio to share his apartment. Then
he had to convince Madeleine to relinquish her treasured
maid, a delicate negotiation, given Madeleine's stately tem-
perament. I have left the story for him to tell, since he is
now living in Los Angeles and several of his scripts have
already been made into movies.

They were together for about four years until Elliot left
Rome. Giglia stayed in Italy, and I think she is back in
Busto Arsizio, properly married, and Sally remained in
Virginia. I keep in touch with the Kaplans' son, Kenneth.
Naturally, because nothing ever changes very much, he
now longs to return to live in Paris or in Italy, and he
wrote to me recently asking whether I knew of a garret.
The notion of a garret seemed a vision as remote these
days as finding the nest of a bower bird, and I wrote back
telling him so. He also mentioned not long ago that Sally
published her book on Mme. de Maintenon, promising to
ask her to send me a copy next time he goes home on a
visit from Princeton. I doubt that she will. The last time I
saw Sally was in front of her house that summer, waving
goodbye. She might have forgiven me for almost drowning
her son, but she did not forgive me Rome.

Maybe Elliot's successes all date back to those years in
Rome with Giglia. He was writing in Italian with such
fluency that he found work as a translator, and began
working on film scripts at Cinecittà. I did not see him
much. Giglia had moved into his murky apartment and
they almost disappeared from sight, immersed in each
other, or so it seemed, and each time Elliot surfaced, he
had gained weight, becoming extremely solid and impos-
ing. Now, when I studied him, I found only quick-sketch
remnants of the school kid wearing braces. I never learned
what happened to Giglia's paintings, but the last time I saw
Elliot before I left on a long trip to meet Jenny at

Dharmsala, he was trying to arrange an exhibition at a gallery on the Via Babuino. Things were going so well for him by then that he might have succeeded.

To formally close the ellipse of views with which this account began, I would like to project one final slide on the screen, and this is of a dinner shared with Elliot just after his arrival in Rome. He had recently moved into the dark apartment with only a few sticks of borrowed furniture and I went there for dinner that week in August, the night of the festival called, in Trastevere, *Noiantri*, We Others, a yearly event across the Tiber celebrated by fireworks and street fairs.

Probably I was gunning for a fight. Elliot had already begun irritating me by telephoning to practice his Italian, which he spoke with a too-perfect accent.

I said, "This place looks like a monk's cell."

Elliot sat solidly on the crate of books he had sent from Virginia. Wearing steel-rimmed glasses, he now looked like a professor in Kraków in the thirties. "It suits me," he said.

"You've been in Rome about ten days and I still haven't figured out what you're doing here."

He shrugged. "Kenneth's gone off to boarding school, and Sally . . . well"—he got up and moved over to the small kitchen—"we've had our good times and maybe they're over, used up. *La commedia è finita.*" He simulated a chuckle. "Remember Tangier? When everything was still in front of us?" he asked. "Well, here I go again. Now it is Rome."

I simulated a chuckle in return.

Elliot said, "Do you know what Edith Wharton said to Berenson about Rome?"

"Not Edith Wharton again," I said aloud, though I might as well have said it to myself.

"She said, '*Why live anywhere else?*'"

"Oh, that's good, Elliot," I shouted. "You know something? I think someone said the same thing to me at dinner in a trattoria last night."

"Take it easy," he said.

". . . or maybe while someone was saying it at my table, I also overheard someone saying it at the next table."

"What are you getting so worked up about?"

"Edith Wharton," I said.

He looked over at me from beneath heavy lids.

But I was not to be stopped. "The phrase 'Why live anywhere else?' does not need a fucking *attribution!* You've been doing this for twenty years. You and your goddamn need for historical reinforcement."

"My historical view of things happens to enrich them for me," he said peevishly.

There was a long pause during which a clock's tick, previously unnoticed, made itself heard.

"Well, well," said Elliot, genuinely surprised, "what if I started in on your defects? The way, for instance, you are clinically unable to see the forest for the trees, or even the trees for the leaves . . ."

By now we were seated at the rickety card table and Elliot, miraculously unperturbed, was carefully portioning out a perfect *penne all' arrabbiata.*

"For instance," he continued in the same old voice, "you've been living in Rome for a long time. Did you know that just beyond that wall"—he gestured with his fork toward the door leading to the barren court—"is a splendid view of the Teatro Marcello, and that the theater itself was converted in the sixteenth century into a Renaissance palace by—"

"—the Orsinis," I muttered, unable not to.

"That was later," he said. "It was the Savellis."

There was a long pause. I poured myself some Lambrusco. This was the kind of zany dispute we had at fifteen, and this was the kind he won.

"Why don't you blast a hole in the wall?" I said after a while. "No one's in town."

He looked baffled.

"To see the view. It's right there, as you say, just across from the wall. You could tear down part of it and no one would know."

"But it's a seventeenth-century wall!"

"I made a terrace out of my roof. It's easy. A few blows with a good hammer and it will turn to dust. Then you can grow a vine around it, and it would look, you might say, like a Piranesi."

Elliot looked at me a long while. "I think something's gone wrong with you," he said.

But after two bottles of wine we did open the wall, unobserved, timing the blows as the fireworks from Trastevere burst overhead in the summer sky. When the spectacle across the river was over, we had uncovered an irregular patch of view the size and shape of a smallish, sleeping bear.

Across the way two Corinthian columns rose out of dark history, the last fragments of the Temple of Apollo. And beyond, illuminated against the sky, was the Teatro Marcello. In the pale light, an elderly creature hobbled over to a fallen capital, its volutes chipped and blurred by a thousand years. On it, two thin cats stretched and rearranged their positions. The figure, wrapped in shawls and woolens even on this August night, was carrying crimson-colored slices of lung brought just for them, her errand illuminating her, transmogrifying her from crone to saint. After spreading this out on old newspaper pages, she left, without demanding from the cats even a caress in return.

I stepped back, satisfied. In saying it was my kind of view, I mean that the one detail humanized the uncontrollably beautiful landscape so that I could possess it. To this day I cannot explain why I persuaded Elliot to open that wall for the view, though I told myself at the time that it was a kind of territorial boasting. Last time I passed through Rome I bought a post card of the Teatro Marcello. In the background is Elliot's opened wall. Many years have passed, but it seems to have been there forever. The vine has slithered across the old stones, and the apartment within, as Edith Wharton might have written in *Roman Fever*, has been entirely restored and belongs now to a countess. And the wall does, in fact, look like a Piranesi.

Waiting for Rita

I guess it was when I found myself in an Irish bar on Third Avenue dimly watching the Academy Award ceremonies that I let myself remember why, a dozen years ago, I finally left Rome.

I had lived in Rome a long time, and it looked as though I might stay on forever, but I was not in love with Rome. More accurately it was a habit, an addiction to the Mediterranean. Most foreigners there during the sixties and seventies had come to Italy and stayed too long. They seemed at the time an unambitious group, particularly the vainer of them who languidly imagined themselves movie stars while sitting at caffès. Although the Italian artifacts lured all of us, and the sunshine and cheap prices were seductive, what we most actively pursued was the all-pervasive promise in the air, the benevolence that cloaked and protected the land.

During my first few weeks in Rome I met a number of people who claimed to be connected to Cinecittà, which they called Hollywood-on-the-Tiber. Most of them, it turned out, were not telling the truth. Everyone in Rome lived partly on lies; the margin between fantasy and reality —so clear in cities like London or New York—was fuzzy in Rome and added to its allure.

One late afternoon I was standing at the counter of the
Caffè Greco, filled at that hour with its quota of Via Condotti society: foreigners, film folk, high-class adventurers,
with a few legitimate Italians mixed in. Someone said:

"Are you American?"

It is an opening line I don't usually like. So instead of
looking next to me, I glanced into the bar mirror to locate
the reflection of the man who had just addressed me. It
was a croupier's face, a croupier in a seedy casino. His eyes
were bloodshot but still sly. Finally I said that, yes, I was
an American.

"You're an actor, yes?"

"No."

"Come on. You're an actor. All tall young Americans in
Rome are actors."

"Oh?" I said, and no more. I looked studiously at the
counter, at the graceful orange and white coffee cups,
edged with gold, for which the Greco was justly famous.
But I had to admit to myself that he was right about actors. They had staked out Rome the way Bedouins do
when they sight an oasis and move in. First one slips over
the dune, then another, then a group of three, three hundred, a colony.

"My name is Gianni Carosi," said the croupier. "I've
lived in America. Here is my card."

He slid his hand into the jacket of his well-fitted, once-
pressed suit and withdrew a shiny crocodile wallet of plastic. I noticed that he had encouraged the nail on his
smallest finger to grow freakishly long, a Sicilian habit
supposed to signify that the bearer of the nail was unac-
customed to manual labor.

"Uh huh," I mumbled, eyeing the card. It was printed with the following:

Mister Gianni Carosi
East 63rd Street, New York

I said, "That's quite an address."
"It's nice, no?" Then he said, "Why are you smiling?"
I shrugged and picked up my coffee cup.
"Isn't it a good address," he asked, "East Sixty-third Street?"
"Sure," I said, finishing my coffee. "Well"—I turned—"nice talking to you."
"Wait a minute," he said, neatly putting the card back in his wallet and his wallet back in his breast pocket.
"Look," I said, not unpleasantly. "I'm not an actor, and I suggest you don't show fake cards to people who happen to stand next to you at a caffè." I said this in Italian and it was difficult for me, particularly the conditional tense of suggest, *suggerirei*. Pleased with myself, I went toward the door where a paparazzo with nothing but time on his hands and a camera filled with unused film took my picture in a blaze of light.
Blinded, out on the street, I crossed through the rush hour traffic to see what jewels Bulgari was displaying in its window. I had never bought a serious jewel in my life and it was unlikely that I ever would, but Bulgari's windows always pleased me.
"So you *are* an actor. They took your picture," said my sidekick, "and you're trying to decide which necklace to give your girlfriend."
When I did not answer, Gianni Carosi of East Sixty-third Street said, "Well, it's true what you thought. I

never lived in New York. I asked someone what would be a good address there and they said East Sixty-third Street, so I had the cards printed. It doesn't hurt anybody. Besides, I always wanted to go to America."

"Then put a house number on the next batch of cards," I said. I looked over at him. He looked back, crumpled. "And keep them in your wallet unless it's absolutely necessary."

"Okay, okay," he said impatiently.

I left him standing in front of the jewels shimmering in Bulgari's window as the crisp Roman sky, heralded by dense clouds of swallows, turned the color of ink.

That was not the last I saw of Carosi. Throughout my stay in Rome he managed to weave in and out of my life, appearing on the scene like a forgetful stagehand. One month he sold real estate, then, all at once, he was a press agent; now he worked in a dubbing studio, now he managed an upstairs travel agency selling cut-rate tickets to Nairobi. Once I was out in noon traffic on my Vespa and I passed an acquaintance of Carosi's going the other way on his Vespa, and so we shouted to each other Vespa-to-Vespa over the fulminating motors, and I learned that Carosi had been picked up on a fraud charge and sent to jail. I thought of visiting him, didn't, and almost forgot about him until one day he appeared at my door.

"I've got a job for you as an actor," he said. "It's a *giallo*, a thriller. You'd play the thief who holds up a bank and gets gunned down on the Piazza Venezia, just below the balcony where that *maledetto* Mussolini made those speeches."

I knew by looking at him that the project would fail. But I also knew that the Roman choreography demanded suspension of belief. So I tried to let him think I took him seriously.

A few days later he sent me a telegram offering me a million lire for the part. A million lire was then about sixteen hundred dollars. He signed the telegram PRESIDENTE IMPERIALE CINEMATOGRAFIA and added a telephone number. When I called that august office, an impatient woman who was clearly Carosi's mother answered the phone. I must have interrupted her just as she was about to put the pasta up to boil, so I left my name and hung up.

"Why do you turn down a film offer of a million lire? A million lire!" Carosi asked. He stood in my doorway, clean-shaven, wearing a new autumn suit of English worsted. The nail of his little finger had again begun to grow long. "Because you don't trust me, right?"

I said nothing.

"A million lire can't be found hanging on a vine like grapes. It will only take two weeks to make the movie. Look at me. I have been prospering. I am a reliable person."

I said, "I've been thinking about it. I don't see myself with a bandana tied around my face holding up a bank."

He said, "But you never *kill* anybody. No one ever *kills* anyone for money in Italy. For love, maybe, or for revenge. This is not America."

"Well, frankly," I began, "I don't see myself ever getting paid the million lire. In fact, somehow I see it costing me money."

Carosi looked shocked. Then he sat down and tapped his fingers on my desk.

"Okay," he said, finally, "I'll be obliged to take different steps, to offer the part to someone else."

"I'm sorry," I began, hoping to be interrupted.

Carosi interrupted. "But I have something else you might be interested in. Why do you make that sound, that sound of fatigue? I'm organizing a banquet. You like to eat, no? You might not like to wear a bandit's mask, but you like to eat. Nice Italian food. A banquet . . ."

"I've got to go back to work, Carosi . . ."

"You'll like this one. It's in a village out of town."

"Hmmm . . ."

"In three weeks. Late October. It will be like a movie. A real-life Fellini movie."

I must have looked interested.

"It's a big banquet. There will be awards. For best film, best actor, best actress. And Rita Pavone will be there to sing! You've heard of Rita?"

I nodded. Rita Pavone was an entertainer who had appealed to the heart of Italy, a freckle-faced girl who sang the last of Italy's girl-next-door songs.

"It's nice of you to ask me," I said warily.

"You'd be perfect."

I said, "Perfect?" Then I felt a click inside my head. "You mean I'm expected to *do* something? It's not just that you're asking me to a Fellini-like dinner in a small town?"

"Would I ask you to drive three quarters of an hour out of town just to eat at a banquet? No! I want to give you an award. A medal. A medal for the best foreign actor of the year. Don't look like that. I've got everyone else. Everyone has said yes, but I'm missing the foreign actor. You're an American. You just have to get up there on the stage, accept the award, say a few words in English, and they'll applaud. Everyone will have a good time. It's in the provinces. Isn't that why you came here? To see Italy.

You don't have to be a *real* actor. You just have to look like one. It's the same thing. It's not dishonest. You'll be, ah, *acting!* That makes you an actor, which, in my opinion —since I am organizing this event—will make you the best foreign actor of the year. So it will be terrific. Terrific!"

In those days I capitulated more easily than I do now, and sometimes I miss the ease with which I said yes to things. Would I now, many years later, drive out of town to an unknown village in Italy, wearing a dinner jacket, to attend a banquet? And would I stand up on a stage and accept a fake award?

How blessed is the Mediterranean! Each year its summer reaches over to embrace the long stretch from late April to early October. Those autumn days were still balmy, and everything was in full flower. At that time— though, as I say, it was just a dozen years or so ago— Europe and America were seriously agitated by rebellion. But not Rome. A few Leftist demonstrations, a few petitions supporting abortion; I joined a straggly march in front of the American Embassy protesting the war in Vietnam. But overall there was the warmth of the sun and the scent of jasmine and the feeling that everything would be all right, possibly tomorrow.

The afternoon of the parade I visited Madeleine, an elegant, long-time friend who lived in splendor above the Piazza di Spagna. She was an elusive person, never quite connecting to her surroundings, and her manner, over the years, had become almost Eastern. But when we met, which was rare these days, her conversation was charming and vague, and just when it seemed to run to foolishness she would say something unexpected and original. The phrase that most particularized her, said through the haze of smoke from her eternal Gauloises, was, *nothing really matters,* which she said not as a lament but as a matter of fact. Sometimes I thought of it as a fine Mediterranean philosophy and at other times it sounded irritating and empty-headed.

We stood against the iron railing overlooking the piazza. The still-strong rays of the autumn sun made translucent ribbons out of the hibiscus petals.

"There's a march tomorrow," I said, "in front of the Embassy."

"That's for you young people," she said. "I'm not much interested in Causes. That's why Rome suits me."

There was a long silence, broken only by the sound of a motor scooter shifting gears as it turned the corner up at the Pincio. I began to say something half hearted about the responsibility we all had, but it seemed pompous even as I finished the first sentence. So I told Madeleine instead about Carosi's award banquet.

"But of course you must go!" she said with enthusiasm, surprising me. "I'd love to go with you and watch you win your award. You can say that you never go anywhere without your mother . . ."

"I don't think . . ."

"Or your sister, if you prefer. I wouldn't mind receiving an award myself, but I can't think of a proper category. It will be like a masquerade."

"You'd go to a masquerade but not to a march," I said. "You don't make any sense, Madeleine."

"I don't intend to," she said, threatening me with a faded geranium she had nipped from a ceramic pot.

And so it was that I decided to accept the award as the Best Foreign Actor of the Year.

The dark comes on quickly in Rome in late October. In the last light the buildings are suddenly in sharp relief, so

vivid and theatrical that they seem imaginary. It is Rome
at its most disturbing. All the unreality hovering in the air
throughout the day is now unavoidable. The light is too
pink, the sky too blue, the surfaces too picture-book clear.
I guess I am saying that it is too beautiful.

I have tried, looking at a map, to remember the exact
name of the town where the banquet was being held. I
know that it was perched along the Via Cassia and I suspect, now, that it might have been called Sutri. But I have
never returned, and if I were to go back there again I am
certain that it will be unrecognizable with new con-
struction, for it was close enough to Rome to have grown
fast. I hope that its name is Sutri, for that is what I will call
it here.

That evening, dressed in dinner clothes, Madeleine and I
drove in good spirits out of town toward the suburbs
where the high-rise buildings had begun to encircle the
city, looming lightless and eerie across the empty fields.
Here and there among the dying poppies and brambly
thickets were occasional farmhouses, lone reminders of an
earlier time when these were cultivated fields.

A wrong turn took us onto a country road hiding
among the carefully graphed suburban outlines. I pulled
over to the side of the road next to some trees and searched
in the glove compartment for a map. By now it was almost
dark. We looked out of the windshield trying to place
where we were, and all at once, rising out of a copse of
trees, stepped a pure white horse with a bareback rider.
The luminous rider and horse seemed for an instant to
float upward, out of the trees onto the road; soundless, too,
as it vaulted the embankment. Then there was a clatter of
hooves on the pavement just in front of our metallic husk.
The rider did not look our way, took no notice of us sit-

ting there in fancy clothes behind the windshield, our heads tilted up in astonishment. Then the horse and rider disappeared into the field opposite, into the sudden night, only the echo of the hooves remaining. It was a memory of eternal Rome, a perishable gift pitched unexpectedly in our path as we were making our way toward a fool's occasion in a town whose name evades me even now.

We drove along the narrow, winding road, passing villages where darkly clothed women stood in their doorways, arms folded, watching, watching, waiting, like the widows of the sea, for the phantom return of their lost husbands. Children rushed through the wide, burned fields, racing with the dark to get home for dinner. Then everything was still. Only an occasional light proved that something lived there. Here and there, like fireflies in the meadows, the farms glowed, promising family warmth, and dinner, and bed. Then there was only darkness, swept by our headlights as we came to a turning, a sign, a sudden clutter of other cars streaming by. The Cassia. It was what we wanted in the first place.

In Sutri we drove up a side street past caffès and vegetable shops shuttered for the night. The town's only restaurant was also its banquet hall; stretched above the narrow street was a banner announcing Rita. Inside the restaurant we were met by the brilliant, unhealthy glow of too many fluorescent lights on too many white tablecloths. Everyone was seated in large noisy groups restlessly awaiting dinner. A table in the center of the room indicated by the majesty of its floral decoration that it was meant for the award winners, and we were led to it by a smiling, unexpectedly debonair Carosi.

Seated next to me was another award winner, a big-breasted woman whose name, if memory serves, was Titi

Medici. She smiled generously and welcomingly. The fullness of her was reassuring, relaxing, and she placed it at the disposal of her tablemates and the public seated beyond at their beaming round tables. I remembered seeing her briefly in a film playing the part of a peasant lady, who ran after and caught a goose, which she then pressed tightly against her bosom, causing it to expire. "It is more humane," I recalled her saying to a farmer who lusted nearby, leaning against his hoe, "than wringing its neck." I was pleased that she was winning an award for this. Of the others at our table, I wondered about their credentials as they must have wondered about mine.

Small children in party clothes ran from table to table, some of them cleverly working their way between our legs and up onto our laps, encouraged by their proud parents parceled about the room wearing their brightest and their best. But finally the abundant plates of pasta arrived still steaming and the kiddies were recalled to their seats to be fed. Despite the chartreuse walls, the fluorescence, the presence of a suspect list of winners, the good-hearted provincial crowd seemed to believe that they were attending a real-life banquet and award ceremony soon to be graced by their favorite singing star. Gianni Carosi had seen to that. He presided over everything. His smile was as white as a schooner's sail and he tacked from table to table making sure everyone was having a good time.

The only problem was that there was no Rita.

Course followed course, platters heaped high, the terminal achievement a tubful of zabaglione that was tilted toward Titi, who ladled it around with a flourish. We had each consumed almost a liter of wine, and we were now sitting in comatose sprawls over our tiny cups of espresso. The good will had begun to pall; so had the animated conversation. The faces, the bloated forms, had turned toward the swinging doors of the restaurant for the entrance of the person they had paid good money to see. But there was still no Rita.

Carosi went up to the microphone in the center of the small stage and blew into it importantly. Then he recited the numbers one through ten several times. "Do you hear me?" he cried. "Yes," came someone's answer, and this dialogue was repeated several times with diminishing enthusiasm. Finally he announced that Rita was on her way, would be there very soon, and that he was now prepared to give out the awards to the accomplished persons who were sitting at the center table. From people used to rising at daybreak, eyes tired, eyes red, eyes lidded scanned our table once again.

A lone photographer positioned himself in front of the stage, crouching, assuring himself of a distorted all-leg, pinhead view of the celebrities. My friend Titi thunked up to the stage, smiled her wonderful smile, grasped Mr. Carosi's hand, arm, medal, with gratitude, joyously suspending her award in the vastness of her décolletée. The banqueters-turned-audience hooted and giggled and applauded with pleasure and it was a tough act to follow.

Carosi was visibly stirred by the applause, thrilled, I think, that his evening was going so well, so thrilled, in fact, that he clearly forgot my name, looking at me with an idiotic blankness that still haunts certain of my dreams. There was a dreadful quiet while everyone waited, while I, too, waited, a semi-smile on my award-winning face while my actual face was hidden under a quilt back in my apartment on the Piazza Farnese.

"But what am I saying?" said Gianni, his carnival huckster's ganglia reconnecting. "Do you know who is standing in front of me? For a moment I was so over-whelmed seeing him in the flesh instead of on the screen, seeing him *not in his robes* but in ordinary clothes!"

He turned to the four disconsolate musicians and said, "Some *Lawrence Of Arabia* music, please!"

He was clearly beyond himself. I do not remember what the band played. I think it was something from *Aïda*, and it played throughout the remainder of my appearance in front of the microphone.

"*Signori e signore,*" he shouted, "Mister Peter O'Toole!"

I think at that moment nothing would have surprised me, so surreal had the evening become. The audience, too, did not seem either surprised or particularly interested in who I was, their minds were so set on seeing Rita. They applauded pleasantly, the microphone, with an enthusiastic flourish, was placed in front of me, and in English I stuttered my thanks to them and Carosi. Almost believing in what was happening, I began an elaborate acceptance speech in Italian. "Would that I could stay longer *a chiacchierare*, to chat . . ." and, rather brusquely, I thought, Carosi eased the microphone away from me and I returned to my seat in a sea of smiles.

The medals had been given out (I still have mine. It is bronze, and on one side of it a heavily clothed woman with wings clumsily ascends; on its reverse side the engraving reads Sant'Angelo d'Oro. I do not know why. I think it must have been a medal left over from another occasion, sold to Carosi at a discount), the coffee had been consumed, the waiters had all left the kitchen and now stood, along with the white-hatted chef, at the edge of the room, to see what would happen next. But nothing happened. Like an ill wind seeping through the cracks in the doorway and the spaces between the shutters, suspicion entered the big room.

To brighten things, an adventurous couple began to dance the polka, and a portly gentleman came over to our table to ask Madeleine, in the most courtly terms, if she would join him for a spin around the floor. Soon she was bobbing up and down, an unlikely figure in turquoise chiffon, her imperious coiffure jeopardized, her expression serene. The other more rustic polka dancers soon stopped to watch, and Madeleine, oblivious to their attention, gamely polkaed onward until Gianni Carosi rushed unexpectedly to the microphone to stop the music.

"I've just had a phone call," he announced breathlessly. "Rita Pavone has had an accident!"

There were assorted sounds of alarm.

"But it's nothing. Nothing. A minor scratch.

An unconvincing sigh of relief circulated around the room and along with it an ominous, impatient rustling.

"Just a small automobile accident nearby. But she will be here in a few moments. Better late than never. Am I right?"

"Yes," said someone near the stage, "you're right."

"And when she comes, she'll sing her great hit, *Il Ballo di Mattone*," shouted Carosi. He then hummed a few bars of the music, the little band took it up, and he walked away from the microphone.

The audience now muttered and mumbled and moved their remaining utensils and glasses about, and I knew that before long there would be real trouble. I also knew that I would leave before it happened. I said goodbye to my neighboring Titi, I signaled Madeleine, and then, nodding to the people around me, I grabbed up my medal and flew to the door, dragging Carosi with me as I went outside.

"You're crazy!" I shouted, in front of the restaurant, struggling to get into my coat. There was a chill in the air. "You're crazy and you should be put in an institution if they don't drag you off to jail."

"Don't be silly," he said.

"Have you taken their money? I mean, have you already put away the receipts of this loony banquet?"

"Uh huh." He patted his plump jacket pocket.

"Then you'd better get out of town fast."

"I can't. Not *now*. Not before Rita comes."

"Look," I insisted, still holding fast to logic, "*you* know and *I* know," I persisted, holding the lapel of Carosi's jacket, "and in a few minutes *they'll* know, that *Rita ain't coming!* That she never was coming. That she's at home in bed somewhere watching television. That she's never even heard of this place or this banquet."

"But look at the fun everyone's had!" he said. "They'll be talking about it in Sutri for weeks. This is a small town. Most of these people have never even been to Rome. They thought their favorite singer was coming here, to Sutri. That's almost the same thing as if she had come. If her little accident means she couldn't come, it doesn't mean she *wouldn't*. SHE WAS COMING! That's enough. When they talk about it, it will be like she was actually here. The night Rita Pavone came to Sutri! Do you understand?"

"Jesus, Carosi," I said, "it's like East Sixty-third Street."

"It's okay. It's okay. I'll tell them the car had troubles after the accident and couldn't get here. I'll tell them that she promised, she promised to come here in the spring. Then I'll serve them some free spumante. I already have it in the kitchen."

"That should make them happy," I said bitterly, turning to go to my car.

"*Esattamente!*" he said, pleased that I understood.

Madeleine had watched all of this very carefully. She extended her hand to Carosi, eased herself into the car, and we drove away.

A chill wind had come up and I shut the car windows and put on the heater, the first time since the past winter. The sudden intense warmth brought back memories of other winters in Rome, of other drives through Italy, and I was overcome by an undefined longing. On the main street, banners announcing the banquet were flapping in the wind, still, announcing the celebrated Rita Pavone. I headed for Rome, driving with my foot hard on the accelerator, speeding past the empty streets of towns I would never know.

"I don't think you belong in Italy," said Madeleine after a long time without speaking. "What I mean is, I don't think you belong here anymore."

I must have turned to her in surprise and anger.

"You see," she continued evenly, "we're each here for different reasons. I think you're sorry you came to that village tonight. You're sorry about the petty dishonesty. Once you start judging everything so severely in Italy, it's all over. Soon you'll complain too often about the traffic, or the fact that the Roman pines are coming down with the blight and no one is doing anything to stop it . . ."

"But it's true," I said at a pitch. "They *are* coming down with the blight and nothing is being done to stop it."

". . . and you'll start to say that the Italians aren't what they used to be, or that they aren't politically involved . . ."

"Well, what about you?"

"I don't care," she said. "That's the difference between us."

There was a long, uncomfortable lapse in our conversation. We were driving along the stretch of the Via Cassia where there were no houses and only a few streetlights.

"Rome is a good place to hide," said Madeleine. "To hide or stay quiet or postpone. It's fine for me. I come, I guess, from the last generation of useless ladies. We were taught how to behave at dinner parties and how to run households . . ."

I said that I did not know what that had to do with hiding.

". . . and we were taught how to dress and how to catch a man, and I did all that. I did it rather well. And one night I was walking home on a quiet street in Murray Hill with a perfect matrimonial candidate, wearing my good clothes and my good jewels, planning (in my mind) the perfect home we would have in Connecticut, and suddenly three men leaped out of the shadows and it was all gone."

I felt my body tense and the steering wheel tighten in my hand.

"My beau—I know it sounds old-fashioned but that is what I called him—was killed as he reached for his wallet, and I was pulled into an empty building just there, where it happened, in the middle of Murray Hill in the summer."

I pulled over to the side of the road and stopped the car.

"No!" she said abruptly. "I can talk about it now without desperation. Please . . ." She touched my arm, urging me to turn the wheel back to the road.

"I did not think that I would ever mend. And maybe I have remained that too-pale, too-delicate figure splayed out in the vestibule. But when I finally left America I never wanted to go back to live, and I suppose I have been a vagabond ever since. I prefer it that way. It makes me

feel safe. So"—she paused—"I do not march in parades
against wars, if you see what I mean. I no longer manage
to fit into a proper category, and it sometimes feels as
though I have become . . . what is that word?"

"An apparition," I suggested.

And I could not know then that one day long after that I
would be visiting her in Istanbul, where she lived as she
had always imagined in a hotel room. From her balcony
there were slanted rooftops and a corner of the Galata
Bridge, now orange-red in the late sunlight. Among the
traffic noises I strained to hear a muezzin chanting from
one of the minarets in the distance.

I said, "I guess you achieved what you wanted. In
Rome . . ."

"Ah, yes, Rome." She lit a cigarette, fanning away the
smoke, and it was clear that Rome had already been
dismissed. "As you suspected, Rome, too, became violent. I
suppose it was inevitable. It took only a few years to de-
stroy all the serenity that was there. But Istanbul is the be-
ginning of Asia. I never tire of wandering through these
imprecise, melancholy streets, and sitting at cafés where
nobody takes any notice of me."

"It doesn't make any difference."

She smiled. "I knew I'd manage to hear you say that one
day!" She said it in triumph.

We had both looked at the darkening sky and back to
the water, and she said, finally, meaning it, "I never want
you to feel sorry for me, for what I once told you about
myself. You must understand that I am now . . . oh, what
is the word? Language is so frustrating, so inadequate. I

seem to speak so infrequently these days that I wonder whether I will finally give it up entirely."

"That you are what?" I asked, realizing with a terrible clarity and sadness how inevitable it was that in some remote place she would one day cease to converse even with a stranger.

"An apparition," I'd said.

I exhaled in a long sigh and drove the car back onto the highway.

"So I don't care about tree blights particularly. Nothing makes very much difference to me . . ."

"Quit saying that!" I said sharply, for now along the dark road, entering the car, came something I can only define as fear. We seemed to be driving in suspended time, in a dream, without moving. The same rubbery streetlamps kept twisting past the car threatening to wrap around us, the same palely lit billboards just about to crumble into dust at the side of the road. Like an irregular heartbeat came the reliable staccato hum from the car's heater. I rolled down my window.

"Everything makes a difference," I said sternly, keeping my eyes on the road. "At least, to me."

"That's why," she said quietly, looking out of the windshield, "I think you should leave."

We drove in silence until we reached the Piazza del Popolo, its twin churches designed, as for the theater, in forced perspective. When I turned to apologize to Madeleine, she stopped me, saying, "I did enjoy that polka. And the look on your face when you thought for a minute you'd actually won an award."

I stayed the rest of the autumn and the winter, but I

carefully left Rome just before the promises I knew would come with spring. I never saw Carosi again. He might have been wrong about those people. He might have been dragged off to jail again, or he might have ducked out and sped away in his car.

Or maybe they believed him.

A Certain Style

Now four of us had settled in a railway car, half an hour early, which is my mother's habit. We put our luggage on the rack at the end of the car near the coupling. The train was going from Rome to Naples. Then we would take a boat to Capri. When we returned to Rome we would meet the others of our group who had traveled elsewhere. It had seemed a good idea, back in New York, to converge on Italy, all seven of us, including my dog. It was a long-cherished notion of mine, of ours, to rent a house in Italy with many friends.

Irene, responsible, said, "You ought to check on the luggage one more time. You can never be too sure."

"Why me?" I asked, anxious to establish at the beginning that in the liberated age my authority was not absolute.

"Because . . . well, I don't really know why," said Irene, her sea-green eyes looking out at the platform. It was 1981. Irene claimed to be a feminist. But she always liked things carried for her, and doors opened, and other attentions once connected to chivalry.

Giulia, well-bred, from Alexandria, whose English nannies had tried to teach her not to speak her mind, said nothing. But her silence came out as a rebuke. My mother said, "Now, how many bags were there . . . ?"

"Traveling with three ladies," I remarked, standing, "is not going to be an easy business."

When I went to check on the luggage there was a gap in the pile, a large gap, an unmistakable gap the size of a piece of luggage. Standing in front of this asymmetrical grouping, I groaned. I groaned not only for the missing suitcase, but in anticipation of the inexorable bureaucratic boredom and red tape that must now fill the space of the stolen object.

"One of them's gone," I said, returning to the seats in a hurry.

I must say for the three of them that their first question was not "Whose?"

"The red one," I said quickly.

"That would be one of mine," said my mother, not surprised, almost as though she expected it.

Giulia rose, her book sliding from her lap. "I'll go with you," she said as I ran to the end of the car and jumped down to the platform.

"A piece of luggage," I said, winded, to the first conductor. "Red. It's been stolen."

"Red?" he repeated. "You're certain it was red?"

I began to shout something. "Yes," interrupted Giulia calmly. "It was red."

The conductor shrugged. There was a commotion somewhere in the distance down the tracks. I saw something red fly into the air. I saw it seized. I saw it hustled away by a gaggle of characters, some in and some out of uniform.

"Hey Champ, it's you!" someone shouted.

I stopped in my tracks.

"*Damn* it, I knew I'd run into you. It's *me*. Eddie. Eddie Random from Studio 54. How many times did I let you past the ropes and crowds? And now you don't know me?"

"Sure," I said. The train was about to leave. The stolen suitcase had just disappeared into the shadows of the train station and Giulia with it.

"I just made a flying tackle at a guy running with a suitcase that wasn't his. You could tell by the way he was running. I got him. The bag popped out of his hands and the police got it. How do you like that for my first day in Rome?"

"I think it's great, Eddie," I said. "The bag's mine."

"*Yours?* A zingy red bag like that?"

There was no time and no need to explain. "Thanks, Eddie," I said, starting to run.

"Call me," he said after me. "You owe me a drink. I'm at the Nazionale with BJ. You remember her. The tall one . . ."

But I was already sprinting toward the *polizia ferroviale*. Giulia, lithe, was already there, toying nervously with a few strands of hair that had freed themselves while running. In the office there were two policemen and a policewoman. Also there was a tiny, nervous man with spaniel's eyes, handcuffed.

"That's the suitcase," I said, hoping to get it over with fast.

"Hah!" cried the policeman, turning to the little man. "And you were trying to tell us it was yours!" Then he slapped the man across the face, hard, once on each side.

Giulia said, "Stop it!"

I said, "Will you just give me the suitcase? Then we can forget the whole thing and you can let this fellow go."

"He's so . . . so small," said Giulia.

"Give you back your suitcase? Let this thief *go?*" echoed the policeman. "You must be mad. This is evidence. We must keep it. We must keep him. And you"— he gestured as though from the operatic stage—"must take another train."

Giulia and I looked at each other.

"He's right. He's absolutely right," put in the policewoman, standing on firm legs.

We'll see," I said, leading them back to the track where our train still stood. The thief stayed behind.

In the compartment, my mother said, "I suppose I don't really *need* anything in that suitcase. I mean, one doesn't *need* a robe, or certain underclothes. I guess I don't *need* to wear my dresses with my belts. Now *why* did I pack all my belts together? What could I have been thinking of?"

"Now, dear," said Irene generously. "Don't start taking it out on yourself."

"We'll stay on the train," said my mother with authority. "Just as planned. We can pick up the suitcase when we get back from Capri." She then dismissed the policemen, who barely had time for an intricate series of low bows and salutes before the train began pulling away from the station.

"Well, I'm glad no one stole our picnic lunch," said my mother, who tends to look on the bright side of things.

Gradually we settled back in our chairs after reassuring each other of how lucky we had been.

"Tackled by a bouncer from a New York disco," I said.

"I thought you never went to that place," said my mother. "That's where everyone smoked cocaine."

"Cocaine is not usually smoked," I said to deaf ears.

Later, we were in the midst of our basket lunch when the train rounded a bend and a port city came into view.

"That's us!" I said, jumping up. We had spread our things over every surface nearby: paper plates, fruit, a mozzarella and tomato salad that Irene prepared, a half-filled bottle of wine, paper cups . . .

"Not at all," said Giulia. She then placed a cigarette into a holder. "We're not due in Naples for another fifteen minutes."

"*Napoli*," came the recorded announcement. "*Stazione Mergellina*." And the train slowed down and stopped.

"We'll never . . ." began my mother.

Plates and fruits flew. We left the wine, we left the bread. The other passengers looked on with amazement as we untangled ourselves, our books, sweaters, and finally our luggage. We had just stepped onto the platform when the train pulled out, taking with it, among other things, my portable backgammon set and a pair of sunglasses.

"We really must pull ourselves together," said Irene.

"I don't understand," said Giulia, "how this could be Naples so soon."

"Do you think we've made a mistake?" said my mother, beginning to worry. "Do you suppose it isn't Naples?"

"It's Naples," I said. "And if we don't hurry we'll miss the boat."

We missed the boat, and while we waited at the pier trying to remain even-tempered, high above us in the sky over the port of Mergellina a hang glider was performing an act midair. The boulevard fronting the sea was choked with traffic, all of it stopped to watch his antics, and every pedestrian was gaping up. It was then that I saw the following: A large Lancia was caught in the stalled traffic, its

windows rolled down, its stylish passengers also looking at
the sky. Adjacent to it, facing in the wrong direction, was
a Vespa. One of the Vespa's two riders—the one not driving—hopped off and crossed languidly over to the Lancia.
He then reached quickly through its open window and removed from the lap of the woman seated there a large
shapeless Vuitton suitcase. He took it with such ease that it
seemed as though he had been storing it there.

The woman screamed, though with the sound of honking and the general crowd noises and Neapolitan holler-
ings, she could not be heard. I knew she screamed because
I saw her mouth open in an oval. The man who had taken
the suitcase then threw it to the Vespa driver, who caught
it like a basketball. He then hopped effortlessly onto the
back seat, and the Vespa, its motor still running, wove
nicely through the traffic and was gone.

My mother said, "Why aren't you looking up? He's
doing wonderful tricks in the air."

I said, "If you had just seen . . . I mean, it's almost as if
. . . I mean, it's becoming surreal . . ."

"What?" she said. "I must say, this is a noisy city."

"I think that's our boat," said Irene, "and we'd better
not miss it."

"Right," I said. "Who knows what wonderful things are
waiting for us in Capri."

"It still amazes me," said Giulia, "that we got to Naples
so soon."

The days on Capri slid by in the translucence expected
of a Mediterranean autumn. The sun was still strong
enough down at the sea to burn us, and my mother sat
veiled under an umbrella. Capri has been granted some
special privilege, avoiding the injuries inflicted on most

resorts, and I suppose if it has endured until now it will be all right for the rest of the century.

Relaxed after a few days, we were anxious to continue our search for a place to live. We had been in Italy for almost a month now, without success. Houses and apartments were so scarce that the classified section of the newspaper listing them had recently been abolished.

But when we got back to Rome we had to begin by retrieving the red suitcase still at the station, for now it was deeply embedded in the machinery of Italian justice. Giulia and I were motioned to an upstairs office, a bleak room with an extravagantly high ceiling and no definable color, where we were told to wait with the same operatic flair that echoed throughout these negotiations.

Our eyes roamed the room. Giulia said, "It's nice to know that the government doesn't throw money away on decorating its offices!" Giulia was in the fashion business and noticed every color, every design, every this and every that.

I paced; then I sat on one of a pair of hard chairs. An official swept in, a man of some importance, judging by the shorter strides taken by the gentlemen with him. We rose, forgetting in our reverence that we merely came to claim a stolen bag. Such is the power of the Law.

"You can identify the bag and its contents?" he asked, easing himself into a chair behind his empty desk. His two subordinates withdrew.

Having decided to say that the suitcase was hers, to spare my mother a trip to the police station, Giulia had rehearsed its contents. My mother, pleased to be relieved of the interrogation, was freed to spend the afternoon shopping.

"I can and will," said Giulia as though from a witness box.

"Ah, these thefts," said the official, rubbing his forehead. "These thefts, thefts, thefts. You catch the crook, put him in jail, give him a sentence. He stays in jail for a month. He's housed and fed. Then he's released, and the following week he's back at the railroad station stealing again. *Yours,* however, was not an Italian. *Yours* is from Chile. We spotted him running with the bag. He's always running. It's not the first time. And he said the bag was his. Imagine, a ladies' red suitcase! He has *always* said the bag was his. *Maledetto!*"

The officer then paused to light a cigarette, sighing as he blew an oval of smoke to the shabby ceiling way above. Then, realizing that Giulia smoked, he elaborately offered her a Nazionale, excusing himself for his lack of courtesy, fluttering his eyelids as he examined what he could see of her over his desk.

"Why?" I began, not certain of my question.

"The laws, the laws, the laws," he said, rubbing his forehead once again. "And the jails are overcrowded as it is. Don't think for a minute that they're all *Italians!* I don't want you to get that impression. We ship the foreign thieves out of the country. Then the next week they come right back in again, driving across the borders, sitting on trains, on buses. There are too many people coming across the border to check each name. They just wave them through. Then they're back here at the station again, stealing." His voice had risen. He seemed about to weep.

"You." He poked his index finger in my direction. "You want to see something?"

I have never managed to say no to that question. On

heavy feet, the magistrate left the office, returning with a thick ledger.

"This is a book of criminals," he said. "Just the criminals caught at this station, mind you, within the past year. They are not all Italians, as you will see. *Many* of them are foreigners."

He opened the book, sighed, and pushed it toward me across the barren desk. Page followed page filled with photographs and descriptions. Faces from Yugoslavia, from Argentina, from the Ivory Coast; faces full of hope, of despair; stupid faces, bright faces, faces unlined and faces ravaged; beautiful faces worthy of the screen and faces so brutal and malevolent that the charge of thievery seemed frivolous.

"Your Chilean," he announced, sliding the book away from me, "will now spend the autumn in jail, all because of a suitcase containing, uh . . ." He reached for his glasses, put them on, and began to read a penciled list.

"We know what's in it," said Giulia. "And we don't really wish to press charges. He seemed so, so . . . small." she repeated once again. "Can't you just let him go?"

The magistrate sighed again. "He'll be gone soon enough, just in time for Christmas pickpocketing. Ah, *povera Italia.*" His hand strayed to his forehead, as though by rubbing it he would rub out the malaise of Italy.

"No one can stay away from Italy. Even the criminals come back again and again," he said with a sigh, easing himself again out of his chair.

He stood, we stood, a subordinate brought in the red suitcase. It seemed such a bright foolish object in that stark room, like a travel brochure on an operating table. It implied another Italy, a sunny Italy of flowers and arches and fountains, with Vesuvius in the background and boats in the harbor and everyone full of smiles.

We got out of there as quickly as we could, haunted by those faces in the ledger, by the desolate office, by the despairing magistrate, and by the forlorn Chilean with the spaniel eyes now in jail because he chose the wrong suitcase.

The official was right. Everyone comes back to Italy. Hadn't I come back as well? But in returning I had to understand that the territory was no longer mine. Rome belonged to none of us who left then. New faces, bright with hope, had taken our place (and we resented them the way we do when sailing past a summer house we once loved, someone unknown to us is mowing the lawn; a dog, on cue, races across the lawn, readying its bark as we pick up speed and move away).

Our small band of weary travelers assembled that evening on the square in front of the Pantheon, all of us in a bad humor except for my dog, India, who sought out the small, sleepy children staring into space while their dripping ice-cream cones—at just her eye level—remained unattended. The reason for our ill humor was the prospect of our homelessness, now that the days were growing short and the nights cool and there was no hearth in sight. During my absence the piazza had become a center for the international caffè life in Rome. In the old days it was the Piazza Navona.

"What about that drink?" said Eddie Random, materializing on the newly revived piazza with his girlfriend.

We added another pair of chairs to our crowded table.

"Rome," he said, raking a hand through his thick curls.

"I could *eat* this place with a spoon. Italy's going to make me famous. I'm designing fashion. Disco things."

"Flash and trash," said his girlfriend, bending down to adjust an ankle strap.

"We've just come from Milan. You know how much money they take in, exporting clothes? Sixty-three billion lire!"

"We've got to get in on it," said the girl, BJ, a tall figure who now threw her head back and looked for the stars. She wore purple makeup, and her blond hair was broom-shaped.

"Seven hundred and sixty thousand sweaters," said Random, hooking his feet onto a nearby chair. "Four hundred thousand pairs of pants."

"You certainly seem to know your facts," said Irene with tact. "Did you know, speaking of designs, that Hadrian is now thought to be the architect of the Pantheon? As though he hadn't done enough!" And here she motioned grandly toward the illuminated temple.

"God, Rome is interesting," obliged BJ.

"I wish we could find an apartment here and now," said my godson Kenneth irritably, not for the first time. He and his friend from Princeton, Chester, had taken a semester off to learn Italian. They looked rumpled, as though they had worn everything in their suitcases a dozen times.

"You've got to try Milan," said Random. "Lots of places there."

"*Milan?*" asked Irene, her eyes still on the Pantheon.

How could we have believed him? But like the petals of some nocturnal plant, we drew our heads together yet again over a caffè table. Milan had always been our last resort. Irene admitted that its libraries might help, since she was preparing a book of recipes from D'Annunzio's time. Giulia, a free-lance illustrator, said she was getting too cold to care where she lived as long as it was heated. Kenneth and Chester pretended to be happy just to be in Italy. And I needed only a desk and some privacy.

My mother arrived on the piazza, rustling with packages, asking us what we were plotting.

"Once again we're thinking of trying Milan," announced Irene. "I had hoped, at first, for a farmhouse in Tuscany."

"Well, that's fine for you young people," said my mother, "but I'm going back to the Gulf of Mexico. For one thing, it's getting too cold. For another, I'm running out of money. I don't know why. I used to come here with so little and make it last so long. And I won't say Europe isn't what it was, because I'm sure that's what *my* mother used to say, so I won't say it again."

And she didn't. She left Italy and went home three days later, while the going was good.

After everyone had gone to bed I took a walk alone, finding myself staring at the Piazza Venezia under the moonlight, a vast, uncongenial space. In the distance I heard a high-pitched howl, a peacock's cry. The terrifying monument to Vittorio Emanuele bared its columned teeth and beamed idiotically from way up high, across from the shadowy mass of the Palazzo Venezia. The rest was a network of boulevards stretching this way and that in a luminous mist to other ends of Rome, past the Forum, past the Colosseum. The wailing melody grew louder, coming from one of the boulevards, joined all at once by a similar sound, like a mating cry, from another direction. They merged, finally, into one piercing siren sound. Two police cars, aiming at the piazza, hurled into view from its opposing sides. The few strollers stopped mid-step to watch. And then, incredibly, the police cars bent on separate errands collided, hitting each other in a broadside that sent them hurtling into the air. They collided as if in a dream, each blue-and-white car spinning lazily around to fly off on a tangent in a clatter of glass and a wounded dragging of metal. One car was now on the sidewalk, the other was jammed against the central podium where, during the day, a white-gloved policeman had stood, elegantly conducting the traffic.

The siren that could not be silenced continued to scream. All the car doors were flung open—all eight of them—and eight rumpled, aching, stooped, angry policemen emerged. Those who had no trouble raising their arms, raised them mightily, gesturing toward their cars, toward the vacantly grinning monument, toward the Vatican way across the river.

The spectators nervously laughed and I laughed too. But I did not have the last laugh, of course, and my retribution came about before the night was over. I continued toward my hotel, passing the eminent façade of the Palazzo Venezia, begun before Columbus discovered America, now known for the bristling speeches Mussolini made from its unoffending little balcony. The narrow streets were empty. But I felt at home, knowing my way in Rome, a city I once loved, resenting the new faces at every caffè. Familiar figures from the past had aged; most of them had not aged well. Those who had owned dogs now walked other dogs, new dogs. I had been gone long enough to have lost an entire generation of pets. But although I was on such familiar terrain, there was something I could not yet define that had seriously altered the atmosphere. It would take me a while before I discovered that the change was an essential one, as surprising as the difference between smooth and rough textures. The velvety seductiveness of Rome was evolving into a coarser indifference. The rhythm, too, had been tampered with: Mediterranean languor now contradicted by a jittery nervousness. Also, altogether new, there was fear.

Fear had never been a consideration. I was aware of it at first because the streets were so empty, piled high with scattering rubbish. Before, so little had been thrown away, so little had been wasted. Then I realized that people turned warily at the sound of my footsteps, a contagion I quickly absorbed, so that I, too, turned; I, too, became suspicious if the car waiting for the traffic light to change did not move on at once. The wall posters all publicized calamities.

I arrived back at my hotel and realized that to avoid a ticket the following morning I must move my car, now parked on the street in front of the door. I started the motor and turned onto the Corso. In turning I noticed a bilious green Fiat parked nearby. Next to it, waving a crimson paddle, stood two young men. They appeared to be waving the paddle at me. I shrugged. I thought they were soccer fans celebrating a victory.

When I turned the car into a small street, a loud siren again started up from somewhere. I do not know why I knew that the siren wailed for me, but I did not slow up for it or stop my car, continuing through the narrow streets to find myself in a dead end next to a hospital. The siren grew louder. I looked apprehensively into the rearview mirror, not knowing what to expect. Then there was a critical screech of tires behind me as the green car swerved around the corner, mounted the sidewalk next to me and stopped abruptly just at my fender. Its doors were flung open; the two men who had stood next to it holding what looked like a paddle jumped out now holding guns. There was no laughter in me this time.

"Your papers!" commanded one of them.

The word *papers* was reassuring, manageable. The gun was at my face. I fumbled in the glove compartment and located the car's documents; then I pulled out my wallet and handed over my license. The guns went back into their holsters. My car keys were yanked out of the ignition. A flashlight now shone in my eyes. As the trunk of the car was being searched, I found my voice.

"What do you want?" I said, my words mired in gravel.

"You didn't stop," said an angry voice behind the flashlight. "Why didn't you stop when we signaled you on the Corso?"

"That isn't a police car," I began, trying to regulate my voice, "and you're not wearing uniforms."

There was an unsettling silence.

"And I thought you were students celebrating the soccer match," I added.

"Some of our best work is done out of uniform," he said, snapping off the flashlight. "In unmarked cars."

"Without uniforms," I began, immediately regretting it, "it's hard to take you seriously."

The flashlight snapped on and off impatiently.

I said, "What are you looking for?"

"Everything," said the one who did the talking, slamming down the trunk of the car. He must have been about twenty or twenty-two. "Arms, drugs, leaflets. We don't have to explain."

He handed back the keys and the documents and began to twirl his gun. "At this hour of the night the streets are unsafe for everybody." His gun once again went into its holster. "You can go."

"But the next time you're asked to stop," said the other one, finally speaking up in a voice tight with authority, "you'd better stop. Just because you're a foreigner doesn't mean you're above the law." His accent was from the hills and poverty of Calabria.

Reversing, screeching once again, accelerating, the green car lunged away to continue its prowling. I sat in my car facing the dead-end street and lit a cigarette.

"Rome," I said aloud to the empty street, to the early-autumn night. I realized that I was rocking back and forth in my seat, my head lowered to the steering wheel, keening, as sure as if something had died.

Just before we left Rome, Random called on Giulia to show her his disco designs and she looked at them with a professional eye. I remember her saying, "Hmm. Bright and sparkly. Like pinwheels." He took it as a compliment, said he'd call us in Milan, and went his way, as we went ours, past the dying towns along the edges of the Abruzzi and Umbria already fringed by autumn, where the last vital villagers have left to make their way in the big cities and only the old have stayed on, hugging the shards of an earlier Italy and waiting to die; past the sweep of the Tuscan hills and north to Lombardy.

PIANTE PERICOLOSE. IN CASO DI VENTO ABBANDONARE LA ZONA, it said on the sign stuck into the dying grass: dangerous plants, in case of wind abandon the area.

Was it an omen? I was sitting on a bench in Milan's public park; India, carrying her leash in her mouth, was tagging after a grime-covered gypsy. The gypsy had just come toward me, beads jangling, skirts flapping, mouthing a series of heavily accented endearments and flatteries in which her clan must have specialized.

"But look at this handsome young man all alone on the park bench. Look how beautiful he is, what a ladies' man, with green eyes of a devil and a mouth that would drive any woman crazy. Doesn't he have a few coins for me?"

I shook my head no.

The big teeth, set in a grin, disappeared for an instant as the lip curled over them. Then the mouth opened again. The teeth seemed to have yellowed as the words spewed forth:

"What a son of a whore, a *froccio*, a bastard too weak and ugly to do anything but sit on a park bench with his pitiful mangy dog." And with that she kept walking.

It was a bad day. The haze had drained the color out of the air for the second week in a row. We could find no place to live. Parceled out all over that bewildering city, the members of our small group were disheartened, threatening to disperse. There were no rental agencies, no ads in the paper for apartments, no friends well connected enough or lucky enough to hear of a half-year lease. We had driven to Como, to Cannobio, to Cernobbio. The following day we were to drive to the Veneto. Each of our excursions had been accompanied by unfulfilled fantasies (a sprawling farmhouse next to an overgrown vineyard, a summer cottage, off-season, not far from a lake, a small house in a village, next door to a bakery). In each of these reveries we would just move in, work on our projects, go for long walks; as evening drew on we would build fires, cook—the kitchens of our imaginations were always large and well equipped. And so on. Instead, I was sitting on a park bench being maligned by a tattered gypsy, staring at a sign warning me that if the wind came up I must abandon the place.

Milan is a city of discouragements. Let me list a few. You are discouraged from walking on the sidewalks because the cars use them for parking. The municipality sometimes tries to discourage this by sinking heavy iron hoops into the cement. Thus you walk into the iron hoops instead of the parked cars. If you notice them in time, the hoops serve to separate you from your walking companion, so that your dialogue—or what can be heard of it over the traffic—is punctuated by shouts to each other as you slalom along. The discouragement does not end here.

You are discouraged, as well, from entering the fortress-like buildings by the heavy doors, the guarded *portieri's* booths, the iron gates beyond blocking the pretty gardens meant for the tenants alone to see. You are discouraged from hearing the service in the massive Duomo cathedral because in the echoing vastness the voice of the priest is halved, by the poverty of the acoustical system, into the present and the past, as though yet another priest with a similar voice is trying desperately to duplicate what has just been said.

And you are discouraged from human contact. The most appealing people are seen blurred, in moving cars, or frozen for an instant next to your own car at a traffic light. In conversation, you are urged to talk about everything but essentials, to discuss your acquisitions, your conquests, your adversaries. At night you stay home if you belong to any social level except what is known as the international set. Then the rules change: fear and caution are thrown to the winds. You are required to go out, continuously, and never to anyone's home. You go out instead in large groups to public places where there is safety in numbers and the overall noise level is certain to discourage any verbal intimacy. But enough, enough, I do not intend to single out Milan for negative comment.

Optimism runs high in Italy. When I think back on that visit to Italy I wonder at our determination. I began to look kindly on my unexpected role of protector, a combination of paterfamilias and tour guide. My itineraries were considered idiosyncratic. With reluctance, my godson and his friend accompanied me to the cemetery, which is there an enclosed city of architectural curiosities. Replicas of husbands and wives lie publicly side by side in bronze Art Nouveau poses; a bronze dog curls up permanently asleep beneath a seated lady's slippered feet. In bronze, too, there are youths on cushions, youths demure and youths monumental, each of them guarded by eternal flames. But the kids, Kenneth and Chester, looked at each other with collaborative irritation, longing, as I would have, at their age, not to consider the matter of death.

One Sunday, Irene and I drove to Asolo, a town perched on the hillsides of the Veneto, so immaculately restored that we found a traffic jam on its main street, caused, we discovered, by a fair of fine antiques. Undaunted by the town's new prosperity, we shamelessly frisked the streets for vacancies. It was in the pharmacy where we learned that a woman across the street actually had a large, furnished apartment for rent.

It was our only affirmative reply in all those weeks.

"An *apartment*," said Irene, as though trying out a new word. We raced to the woman, arms outstretched, with the pleading look doomed lovers are said to have.

"Well," said the fine-boned landlady, wrapped securely in many sweaters, with skin of a bluish hue, "here it is!"

She made a wide, magnanimous gesture at the doorway

of the available apartment, offering it to us like a silver service for twelve.

"It's yours," she said. "Most Americans are leaving Italy, you know, because they get taxed here and they get taxed back there, both, or so my other tenants have told me. I'm pleased to see that there are still those among you . . ."

"Is there a kitchen?" asked Irene, her hand on her hip.

"You will have to pay extra for the use of the kitchen. It is on the floor but it is separate."

"Ah."

"And the furniture?" I said, standing behind one stark chair.

"At the rent I'm asking I don't think you ought to expect . . ."

"But we thought it was furnished," we said together.

"It's furnished. It's furnished. Aren't you leaning against a chair?"

"And the heat?" I asked uselessly.

We were at the door.

"You saw the frescoes?" said the woman, blocking our way. "They are in perfect condition. Not like those frescoes that fell on your ambassadress in Rome and poisoned her, little by little."

"That was before your time in Italy, dear," said Irene to me. "Clare Boothe Luce, just after the war. This woman has a fine memory."

"I'm sure she's a fine landlady."

"I've got another place nearby," shouted the woman, calling out to us as we rushed back down the stairs and into the street.

"I'd rather be in Hoboken," said Irene when we found ourselves in the town's fanciest hotel ordering a drink. It was dusk. We knew that there would be no apartment, no house overlooking the surrounding countryside, and we knew that we did not belong in a manicured town in the Veneto. We were anxious to leave, attacked by what might be called a traveler's angst, when the time of day (usually nightfall), the place, and the general atmosphere combine to cause a seizure of alienation. Fortunately, we both felt it at the same time, and we have known each other so long and so well that it did not have to be mentioned. Our eyes were darting around the near-empty hotel lounge. We looked out into the oncoming, homeless night, gulped our drinks, paid, rushed to the car, and fled the town.

"Maybe some institution will take us in," said Irene.

"Maybe we'd better go back."

"Go back where?"

I stared through the windshield and started the motor. "Maybe we'd better go back to America and be done with it."

Eddie Random had called my hotel a few times while I was away. Each message was marked *urgente!* I heard myself muttering, *pushy little bastard*. I was prone in recent weeks to mutter such unpleasant comments, an obvious signpost on the bleak road to senility. I decided, rashly, independently, that what I needed to refresh my spirits was a week alone in Switzerland.

If you wish to see a town's poor, travel through its deserted streets and wander around its depots at dawn. With a fringe of mountains, in the earliest hours of the day, Milan looks like a frontier town. There is no sign of its prosperity. The morning I left for Switzerland the empty streets were punctuated by workers bicycling to their jobs in the rain, holding unsteady umbrellas in their free hands. The streets shone in the early light like lagoons. At the head of a wide boulevard the immense railway station loomed like a monument to the colossal aspirations of the thirties. The single word FASCIS dominated the cornice, artfully obscured, in part, by time.

Pigeons fluttered upward as the trains pulled in under the vastness of the glass roofing. If the mist and steam did not rise from the tracks in fact, they were there in the imagination. I had planned on driving to Switzerland. But the previous morning when I went out for my first coffee I discovered that, during the night, the wheels of my car had thoughtlessly been removed. The magistrate (another magistrate, another city) threw up his hands: *persone ignote*, he had said, persons unknown. *Maledetti!* he added, as they always do, his eyes scanning the ceiling.

Pulling open the door to my train compartment, a well-dressed, pale woman stepped inside without meeting my eyes. She noted that all the seats but mine were empty. Then she slowly removed her gloves, throwing each one onto a seat to reserve them both. A stout man then entered the compartment, a soft felt hat on his head, nattily dressed. He looked at the two gloves, stared at them. Then he decided on one of the vacant seats, sighing into it, as though he had long awaited this moment. Now the woman returned, looked at her two gloves, and sat anxiously in one of the two seats she had claimed, removing her glove from the other seat as well. Lighting a cigarette, she puffed on it nervously while the train moved out of the station into the rain and cold of late autumn. The mountains in the distance were now obscured by fog. The woman suddenly snuffed out her cigarette in the ashtray concealed in the armrest of her chair. Abruptly, she stood, opened the compartment door, and disappeared into the corridor, never to return.

"*E un mistero,*" said the man in the felt hat seated opposite me. "*Una donna scomparsa . . .*" A woman disappears . . .

I smiled. It seemed to be the beginning of a spy film of the forties.

The man then looked into the ashtray where the cigarette butt was still sending a plume of smoke into the air of the compartment. He looked over at me again. He then inspected the vacated seat and the area beneath it.

"What are you looking for?" I asked, unable not to.

"Aha! you never know," he said, finally sitting back in his seat. "You never know about anything these days. Quite honestly, *onestamente,* I was looking for a bomb."

I rustled my newspaper.

"Of course, if you're foreign, as I suspect you are, then you cannot understand. I am fearful all the time."

His tone was almost boastful. He studied me from time to time during the train ride. Finally, deciding that I was an acceptable recipient of his confidences, or unable to resist telling them, he said, "My brother-in-law was kidnapped, you see. The family had to pay three hundred million to get him back. He has gone to live in Paris."

Then he reached over and snapped my newspaper with his index finger. "In today's paper there are two."

I had just read about the two separate kidnappings that day: a girl on her way to a riding academy and a young chemistry student, both children of local industrialists. Also, published almost daily in the newspapers like stock market quotations, there is a list of recent kidnappings: who, when, how much money demanded, whether the

money was paid, whether the kidnapped person had escaped, died, or vanished. To date there were ninety-four
of them in the area of Milan. Only some of the victims had
been returned.

He said, "So I look in ashtrays. Imagine! It's come to
that."

At the station in Lugano, after the other passengers left
the train, the stocky man from my compartment stepped
onto the platform, where he was suddenly flanked by two
men who ran alongside him. I began to shout as they el-
bowed him into a black car at the curb, but as the driver
leaped out to open the door, I saw that the men were his
bodyguards. The car sped away from the curb and the
man, turning, waved goodbye.

The orderliness of Switzerland served only to make me
realize that its absence, in Italy, was disturbing, that the in-
tent of both the Far Right and the Far Left was total dis-
order, anarchy, change at all cost. It was the mindlessness
of it I feared. At the border the passengers were asked to
get off the train. This was surprising because it was an ex-
press train to Milan, but we discovered that there was a
strike of the railroad engineers, a twenty-four-hour work
stoppage of the kind that has plagued Italy for the last two
decades in every public area of life. And so we were
required to pass through the customs house in a long file,
and everyone grumbled, the customs officials as well.

Ahead of me an Italian woman was asked how much
money she was carrying with her and she said quite dis-
tinctly, "Thirty thousand lire," which was more or less the
amount allowed. Then the customs man asked her to open
her pocketbook. She unsnapped the clasp, lit a cigarette,
and I realized that it was the same woman who had come

into my compartment on the train to Switzerland and then disappeared. Now I had a chance to study her more carefully. She had auburn hair, neatly arranged, and looked like a prosperous businesswoman who might have run one of the small industries in northern Italy, and nervousness seemed out of character. I stood back and let the other passengers move ahead of me while I tried to watch her without seeming to.

"And this?" said the customs inspector. "This is a bank statement?"

"Yes, it is clearly a bank statement," she said. She seemed appalled that it was there. "But it is not mine."

"Not yours? Not yours?" He looked impatiently at the next person in line. "Over there," he said curtly. "Move along. There is another inspector."

"No. It belongs to a friend."

"You carry a bank statement for sixty million lire that belongs to a friend?"

"My name is not on it," she said.

"No one's name is on a Swiss account," he replied. "But there is a number. We can check the number."

"You will find nothing to implicate me," she said bitterly, and it was then I realized that she had brought the money from Milan several days before—acute nervousness accounting for her behavior in the train compartment—to open a bank account in Switzerland. Returning to Italy, the woman had foolishly kept the statement in her pocketbook. Now, smoking frantically in front of the customs inspector, she must have realized that it was too late.

"I am sequestering this," he said, his voice rising in pitch. "We will now proceed to inquire about this account. In the meanwhile you will be required to post five times the amount of the account with the government."

"Five times!" she cried. "It isn't possible!"

"It is routine," said the inspector. "You!" He now pointed in my direction. "What are you standing there for? Are you spying on our conversation?" he shouted. Then he turned to the woman and said, "Is this man with you?"

She turned to look at me. "I do not know him," she said. "He has nothing to do with this."

"Then get going," he said, motioning me along.

When she turned back to the desk she threw her cigarette onto the floor, stepping on it savagely as they began to go through the story once again, the officer outlining the procedures and penalties that now awaited her. The bitter encounter suggested the grim, choleric reality of present Italy.

Giulia met my train. She was wearing a warm coat with a fur collar and she slid her hand into the cuff of my short leather jacket.

"We all missed you. The weather has been dreadful. And wait till you hear the rest."

"It can't be that bad. At least I didn't have to leave three hundred thousand dollars at the customs shed."

"What?"

"I'll tell you later. Now you tell me your news."

"You never called your friend Random back, did you?"

I shook my head. "I had enough troubles."

"He called you every day. He said it was urgent. He found a huge apartment."

"Don't tell me the rest."

"But . . ."

"It's too late," we said in unison.

"He's taken it himself. He's signing a good contract designing those dreadful disco clothes. He arranged it in

Rome. They're thinking of including licenses in Japan . . ."

I said nothing.

"Funny," she said, "I had a feeling he might catch on. The fashion business is so, well, capricious."

"I should have known when he tackled the thief," I laughed, "that he had talent."

Outside the station a light rain misted the air.

"They've invited us to dinner this Friday," said Giulia.

"That's very kind. A home-cooked meal."

"BJ's bringing over her family for Thanksgiving. The place seems to be immense . . ."

I interrupted her. "Now let me amuse you with my tale about a mysterious woman on the train."

There are many specific situations about which I am hopelessly vague, and although I regret my poor memory, I am also surprised by the odd assortment of artifacts it retains intact, awaiting only the most rudimentary trowel to lift them into the present.

And so on Friday evening, defeated, we collected bitterly at Eddie Random's newfound apartment. When we were seated at the dinner table, I looked around at our gallant group and realized, finally, how clownish we were to have imagined that we could have fit organically, now, into Europe. All we needed were funny hats and noise-makers to complete the spectacle. It was at that moment that I remembered an isolated incident at a childhood birthday party, a fancier party than we children were then used to. Someone had dropped a crystal goblet on the floor, breaking it. I remembered it because, although I was not the child who broke the glass, I had been blamed. I was punished in front of the other children by the birthday boy's mother (maintaining my silence) and I resolved that one day I would be grown up and that I would thrillingly break my own fine goblet to even the score.

But I have not described Eddie Random's miracle apartment. It was actually an apartment-showroom belonging to an American fashion designer who had suddenly left town under a cloud. He was known mainly for his "bird" prints, and the rooms were filled with them, flapping across the walls, the windows, the carpets. Where there were no birds there were his initials, linked. The remaining vacant spaces in the rooms, which might have once exhibited portraits of the Sforzas or Beatrice d'Este, held enlarged advertisements featuring the designer himself, carefully edited into a pair of blue jeans of his own make, with a sea gull clutching those initials stamped onto the back pocket. I was told that the designer was in professional trouble, and although he had come to Italy in the late forties as a young man of looks, talent, promise, and ambition (a combination then irresistible in Europe), he had stayed on too long, clinging like a barnacle through thirty-nine changes in the Italian government.

"Change," Random was saying. "That's what my clothes are all about. The present. Now."

"I'm getting into the business, too," offered BJ, passing around a large, cooked fish. Her hair had changed color and was now mainly orange. "I'm eager to try the jeans market. My initials cry out, *BJ's Blue Jeans!*"

"Well, I suppose they do," said Irene.

"We love Italy," said Eddie Random.

"*Really,*" said BJ.

Kenneth made an unpleasant, peevish sound with his lips.

"I guess I don't care much about clothes," observed

Chester. Then, on reflection, he added, "Well, maybe that's not altogether true. I like LaCoste shirts."

I thought: We are in Europe. Why do we bother to come here anymore? The thought had begun somewhere in my toes and was spreading up, up . . .

"There's fashion even in the churches," said BJ. "I was looking at the bones of St. Ambrose just the other day, underground, in a crypt. He's been dead for *years!* But he's wearing golden slippers, a lilac robe, and little red gloves."

Ambrose: the man who baptized St. Augustine, flanked by two tall Roman soldiers, their bones the color of burnished walnut, interred and exhumed throughout one thousand years, the stark brown bones surviving barbarian invasions, the Middle Ages, Prospero embarking from Milan's gates, Spanish domination, German, French, Austrian occupation, Verdi's death, and a public hanging, by his toes, of Mussolini and his mistress, from the girders of a garage in the center of town. Ambrose, finally at rest behind glass.

"It's this *town*, man," offered Random. "They wear chinchilla-lined raincoats."

Giulia sighed. "Concealed chinchilla. The idea is to pretend to hide the fact that one is rich. Only foreigners wear out and out *furs*." She sat back as though exhausted by her comment and placed a cigarette in her ebony holder. Her food remained untouched.

Kenneth said, "Which one's chinchilla?"

"The expensive one," said Irene. "You needn't concern yourself."

"Ah, what I've been trying to say is . . ." I began, desperately hoping to hold on to a thought, "is that we keep coming to Europe and coming to Europe, but we can never *become* Europeans no matter how long we stay."

The table seemed unnaturally quiet.

"But when foreigners come to live in America," I added, "they're absorbed without a trace."

Giulia said, "Thank you," as Random lit her cigarette.

"Speaking of being absorbed without a trace," said Irene, "will you pour me some more wine? I know it says Frascati on the label but it probably *isn't*. They've taken up calling any white wine Frascati."

Kenneth said enthusiastically, "There was a big wine scandal last year in Sicily. They were bottling bull's blood mixed with alcohol. I wish I could remember what they called the wine. On the label, I mean . . ."

It was then that I hurled my glass across the room. I wonder, now, what made it happen, whether it was because I hadn't been heard, whether the conversation was so irritating, so full of foreigners' quibbling, or whether it was the goblet itself, so carefully etched with interlocking initials, so elaborately, expensively carved out of crystal, a perfect set of twenty-four, judging by the army of them on the sideboard, of such fine quality that by shattering only that particular goblet would I adequately fulfill my childhood dream of grownup revenge.

No one at the table spoke. The birds on the walls, stalled mid-flight, seemed to make a rustling sound as we looked around the table at each other in the candlelight, and we were left to interpret the incident as we chose, as a reproach, as a sign of madness. Or as an end to something. And in the aftermath of the theatrics I think we each remembered how we had imagined it would be, seated around a similar table in New York, when we planned this trip, looking ahead to Italy.

"And before it's too late," I said, when things had calmed, "does anyone else want to get out of this place?

Because as soon as the wheels get put back on the car I'm leaving for France."

We sat on the terrace in Menton looking back at the shining curve of Italy along the Mediterranean. The trip had taken a day. The fog was so dense in Milan that the toll-booth collectors had gone on strike, and the phantom line of cars pressed forward as though seeking illumination elsewhere. At Genoa we saw the first palm trees, sensed the warmth. Then, speeding and twisting around the curves and under the tunnels, we got to France. Now it was night.

We checked in at a hotel along the seafront, not minding that the proprietress had no charm, that we had left charm behind. We took India to the beach, past the posted French interdiction, allowing her a run along the coast. She ran, as deranged with happiness as we. The euphoria was unreasonable, wounding because we knew we could not make it last, that a foreigner so refreshed to find himself in civilized France after unruly Italy might be that same foreigner who later feels released from France's unyielding strictures into Italy's vivid commotion. That same evening, a group mirroring ourselves might be seated in awning chairs opposite ours in Ventimiglia, looking across the coast toward France—shimmering as it spreads out toward Monte Carlo—a group as happy as ours to have crossed the border.

And the Italians, the French, mindless of the foreigners' drama, continue to live against their familiar backgrounds. It is the aliens who cannot properly connect, who judge and generalize and bother worrying where they feel at home. Their apartness is as permanent as Burton's was in Arabia, and all their languages, their disguises, their careful

investigations, can never fuse them to the place no matter
how they long for it.

By the time we got back to Milan, I had found a small
house in France and I only had to wait two weeks to move
into it. By then, we would have each gone our separate
ways. It was almost December. Irene had decided to return
to New York, her D'Annunzio only half finished, her fund
of Italian recipes untried. Kenneth and Chester had lost interest in studying Italian and wanted to leave for Greece
before their new semester. All of this was determined in
the cramped car driving back to Milan. Once again we
were enveloped in fog. The toll-booth attendants had gone
back to work. Instead of change, they filled our palms
with hard candies. The collector smiled, his eyes roaming
over each of us in turn. We were back in Italy.

The snow drifted down and the air around the Duomo
was perfumed by truffle stands. When the snow let up the
fog came back. Giulia found herself a one-room apartment
on the Piazza San Babila. Left alone, we took walks along
the chilly canals trying to imagine what Milan was like
when boats arrived there from Venice. Now that I was
leaving I found Milan almost beautiful.

The last night before I left we decided to celebrate and
Giulia dressed herself in one of her 1940s cocktail dresses
that rippled even when she stood still.

"Schiaparelli," she said in a haughty voice. "It will be
around long after Eddie Random has left Italy to run a bar
in Tallahassee."

"How do you know anything about Tallahassee?"

"I don't," she said. "I like the word." She then added a
piece of her grandmother's jewelry, a heavy gold and dia-
mond pin in the form of a leaf, from other times in Alex-

andria. She studied it in the mirror, removed it, hesitated, and finally pinned it once again to the dress when she saw me look at my watch.

"My mother always told me to remove the last thing I put on before going out," she said. "Why are you always in such a hurry?"

"We made a reservation."

"But this is Italy," she said, studying herself one more time in the mirror. "You sound as though you've already left for France."

We drove through the foggy streets as though prowling. Something glowed in the distance, a yellowish vapor clotting the streets up ahead.

"Milan's burning," I said.

"Terrorists," said Giulia, as though it explained everything that went wrong.

Flames illuminated the buildings. Imprisoned in the traffic, we had to stop the car near the giant square. The Duomo itself had become a massive, clawing temple, as vast shadows leaped across it's Gothic façade. We got out of the car and squirmed through to get a better look. A parade circled the piazza; thousands of workers streamed through from the Via Manzoni carrying torches. The police encircled the Galleria.

Fascisti carogna
Uscite dalla fogna*

Hammering on the car hoods with nightsticks, the police compelled the drivers to back away from the square. Giulia and I were wedged into the zigzag aisle of jammed cars until we found our own. The shouting, the

---

* *Fascist carcasses, come out of the sewers.*

honking horns and policemen's whistles, were now joined
by small explosions ricocheting off the baroque palaces
lining the street. When we finally managed to drive
through the narrow pavements we lost our way in the
fog. By a miracle we reached the mists rising from the
canal, and the small lantern outside the restaurant beckoned
like a treasured friend.

Inside, the atmosphere was cheerful. The Milanese regu-
lars waved to each other and nodded, pleased to have this
refuge. On the muted tape, Endrigo's *Elisa* was playing.

> *Sono rimaste poche stelle*
> *E stan cadendo ad una ad una*
> *Il bimbo ha perso l'aquilone . . .* *

Guilia said, "It's beautiful, this song, no?" with the habit
she had, a habit shared with the English, of asking at the
end of an opinion whether you approve.

"It's really an incredible language," she continued. "I
mean, think of *aquila*. It means eagle. But you can say
aquilino, and it's little eagle. You can say *aquilaccio*, and
it's a horrible eagle . . ."

The haughty look had gone. Even in her Schiaparelli she
seemed emphatically vulnerable, the way she had looked in
the magistrate's office in Rome.

"*Aquiluccio*," I began, "adorable little eagle . . ." But
the full sentence never reached the air.

"LE MANI IN ALTO!" *Put up your hands!*

The shout came from behind me where the door was.
Giulia's face had frozen into an expression that had nothing to do with fear. It was simply her earlier expression,

* *Only a few stars remain*
And they are falling one by one
The child has lost his kite . . .

still involved in her discussion on semantics, immobilized, mortuised.

"Don't turn around," she said between her teeth.

But I did turn around, of course, to see three gunmen standing at the entrance of the restaurant with masks of red cloth covering their faces. Their guns were pointed at the semicircle of the room, and the quiet in the room was absolute. Only the tape continued, the husky baritone voice singing of a lost love.

The shout was repeated. "*Le mani in alto!*" The second time it sounded almost reasonable.

Neither of us obliged. I think if one of us had raised his hands the other would have followed, and I cannot even explain now why we left them there on the table like discarded objects. I think that the accumulating insanity of the evening lifted us out of our seats and we rose in our minds to the ceiling to become spectators watching from some distant place.

Quickly two of the gunmen crossed the room while the third man waited at the door, his gun moving nervously in all directions. "Don't move!" he repeated. "Don't move, or I'll shoot this gun without hesitating."

The silence was now complete. Either the tape had been switched off or come to an end. One of the gunmen's shoes squeaked as he strode from one table to the next, grabbing the wallets and purses that were wordlessly handed to him. The other man was a few feet from our table when the gun went off. The bullet nicked the desk where the proprietor stood, his hands trembling in midair.

"If you call the police, you're dead," said the man at the door, his gun again pointed at the tables.

The man passing near us grazed and knocked over a third, empty chair at our table. Unobscured by the red mask, his phantom eyes passed across Giulia, noted her gold pin, our immobilized hands, my suit, my eyes (as I looked back through invisible opera glasses and saw his fear magnified). He stooped to pick up the chair and passed us by. Then he was at the next table taking their valuables. When the man at the door said at a pitch, "*Andiamo!*" the three gunmen converged at the door. In their haste there was an instant of comedy confusion about getting through the doorway, but then they were gone in the fog, as thick there as though a machine was churning it out next to the canal.

There was a long, long silence in the restaurant. Then all at once a combination of shrieking and wailing shot up from the tables, the sudden noise as shocking as the quiet during the robbery. The owner of the restaurant phoned the police; twice his unsteady fingers failed to dial the number. The policemen arrived, strutting in in black boots, handsome as thoroughbreds and aware of it. They did not rush back out into the foggy streets. Instead, they stayed to comfort the shaken, to hear the various versions of the story now told in screams by the diners, and the music tape, though turned back on, could not be heard.

"Did you notice?" asked Giulia, regaining her voice. "Did you notice the way . . . the way he left us alone?"

"Naturally. Naturally I noticed," I answered, too harshly.

"No," she said, irritated. We were both now in a nervous state with all the confusion around us. "I don't mean, 'Did you notice *that* he left us alone.' I mean *the way* he did it. I've always suspected all the crimes in Italy of having an element of, well, you know how the Italians are. There was something just now . . ."

"You mean, *the way* he didn't take your pin, *the way* he didn't grab my wallet?"

"The way he picked up the chair. The way he *spared* us," she added, still puzzled. "You've got to admit that he had a certain . . ."

"A certain style?"

"Well," she said, beginning to laugh, the fear and nervousness slowly leaving her, so infectious that it crossed the table and carried me along. I leaned over and traced her laughing mouth with my fingers.

"Well, yes. A certain style," she repeated. "You see . . ." she began, her opened palm serving up the room, and Milan, and the peninsula reaching south of us into the soul of the Mediterranean. "This . . ." She might have been Victoria extolling the virtues of the Empire. "This is *still* Italy, after all."

The
Lady Who Lived
in the Woods

Before I ever lived in the South of France, I passed through it on my way elsewhere, thinking only that it was a playground for the rich and not meant for the likes of me. I was very young then and thought in broader terms than I do now. As it turned out, my reading of the place was fairly accurate, though incomplete. I was traveling then with a friend from college, Michel, whose Swiss parents owned a villa in the hills between Cannes and Juan-les-Pins. It was called the Villa Cleopatra, and it was not far from the Château de l'Horizon owned by the Aga Khan, a mysteriously blank building pressed between the railroad tracks and the sea.

The Villa Cleopatra had an extensive garden filled with rare plants, trees, and bushes, and Michel's father, an important watch manufacturer, had taken great pains to illuminate various sections of it. At night, after dinner, he would stand next to a complicated battery of light switches, and along a back wall, a cascade of bougainvillea suddenly swept into view. Now the banyan tree arose, a somber cathedral in the deep center of the garden, only to vanish again into darkness while a small army of cactus massed on the hillside.

But my main memory of Michel's father was that he

was having *an affair*. Michel's mother was extremely beautiful. In a room, she seemed to place herself physically closer to us than any of our other friends' mothers did, and her "sweetheart" necklines revealed palpable substance for our most ardent dreams. I had difficulty imagining why her husband was unfaithful: clearly it was she who should be having the *affair*. Michel, his mother, and I were at lunch one day in Mougins, a hill town above Cannes, and at a nearby table, by accident it seemed, sat his father with his lady friend, a less pretty woman even younger than his wife. Just before leaving the restaurant Michel's mother went over very pleasantly to her husband's table, greeted him, smiled at his friend, and then said to her husband, running her crimson fingernails through his sparse hair, "Darling, what a surprise! I meant to ask you this morning: Did you remember to take your suppositories last night?"

I thought at the time that this was very sophisticated, in fact that it was the most sophisticated remark I'd heard, and typical of folks who summered on the Riviera.

I assume that Michel and his family were appropriately well connected and rich, though this idea alone did not give rise to my speculations concerning the Riviera. I assured myself that I did not care about villas and yachts and the rest of the paraphernalia there and went on to join a friend on a trip to dour Spain. Meanwhile, the Riviera thrived.

Several years later I inherited a small amount of money from a much-loved aunt, and I bought a French station wagon with it and drove south from Paris. It rained during most of the trip and by the time I got to the coast I regretted having decided to visit France in the winter. The Mediterranean was whipped by high winds as I drove along the Grand Corniche, and by the time I had curved down to the coast the waves had crossed the narrow beach between Juan-les-Pins and Cannes and the boulevard was covered with water. I passed the Château de l'Horizon once again, its grey-white wall the only solid mass among the furiously waving palms, and on an impulse I cut sharply off the road and drove up to the Villa Cleopatra, or where I thought it would be. Nothing stays the same, I said to myself, not for the first time.

In recent years I had lost touch with Michel and his family, but I was unprepared to find that the Villa Cleopatra was no longer there. In its place, extending into the garden and obscuring most of it, was a bright square condominium advertising itself as Les Sables d'Or, with three- and four-room apartments for sale. I must have suspected then that this incursion into the hills of the French coast was only a beginning. But what saddened me was that Michel's family had probably broken up along with the carefully lit and dramatized garden, and instead of concerning myself with the deteriorating Mediterranean, I pondered personal loss, and times gone by, as I drove disconsolately into Cannes, thinking that it was about time for me to get out of the car to find a suitable café in which I could nurse my sudden sorrows.

I turned the corner and pulled into a parking place along the Croisette, intending to go into the Festival, a favorite café of mine during the summer I had misprized the Riviera.

"Are you the fellow who was supposed to see the farmhouse, or I should say *mas*, which is what they say here, at four-thirty?" asked an Englishman with a pencil-thin mustache as I stepped onto the sidewalk. "Because if you are, we've got to hurry before it's too dark."

I looked at him, noting that behind him, next to the café, was a real estate agency. I said, "What was his name?"

"Well, I mean, you're either *him* or you are not *him*, aren't you? And, you know, if you *are* him, you would know your name, wouldn't you?"

"Does one say *him?*" I said. "Or *he?* I've never really known." He did not hear me.

"Did he say he'd be driving a Simca station wagon of deep maroon?" I asked in a louder voice, pointing with my thumb to the car I had just parked.

He said with suspicion, "Nao."

"Then what made you think that . . . ?"

"He was *American*, you see, and you are an American, judging by your red TT plates, and he was to meet me here at four-thirty. He, or you, are a half hour late. Look," he added impatiently, "I don't see why we're doing this elaborate rondelet . . ."

"To give me time to think," I said with honesty. "And now that I've thought about it, I think it's a good idea. Let's go and see the farmhouse or, as you say, the *mas.*"

The agent, named MacGrath, was a bit bewildered, and my own mind was spinning with this unexpected turn of events, and so the only words we exchanged on the twelve-minute drive to La Roquette sur Siagne were about the beastly weather and the fact that it was a relief the summer was long over with. The windshield wipers of his car did not quite manage to clear the floods of water that came toward us and dripped through the window edges.

Finally he said, "You'll like Olive, if she's in, though she's not particularly hospitable. You know how it is with Englishwomen of a certain age. They want really to do nothing but garden. The garden up there has everything from, ah, anemones to . . ."

"To zinnias," I suggested.

He chuckled.

I said, "It must be wonderful in the summer."

"Even now," he sighed. "Even now."

I decided I liked MacGrath.

"She only wants to let it for four months, you see, starting in May. But perhaps," he said, sliding his eyes in my direction, "I've already told you that."

We had driven into deep countryside as soon as we left Cannes. In the distance rose the Maritime Alps, and perched on a nearby hill was Mougins, where Michel, his mother, and I . . .

But to keep myself from falling into the ready trap of nostalgia, I watched the countryside. Even in the rain it was the landscape of dreams, gently rising from the seacoast in graduated waves toward the low mountain range.

"Well, this is it," said MacGrath. "This isn't the *village* of La Roquette, actually. This little place here is sort of its suburb." He tittered pleasantly as we drove on a small country lane with several stone houses strung along it. The mud stretch came to an end in a large field; just before it we swung off to the left and into a small hidden driveway.

I must have thought, during the rest of that year and into the following spring, that I had dreamed up the farmhouse in the South of France to compensate somehow for the loss to the cosmos of the Villa Cleopatra. But my imagination could never have supplied the details. It was called the Mas Katia and I suppose it fell into some non-category, being neither a proper farmhouse nor a villa. It was set in a small olive grove and made of the local stone. The newer parts were stucco, painted in a tawny pinkish hue. In the rain, at that hour, the flowers that still grew there, even in the autumn, seemed illuminated from within.

"Well?" said MacGrath.

We had stopped in front of its door. Just next to it, in a giant ceramic olive jar as tall as a man, grew a rambler rose, covered with bright blooms, curving over the outside staircase to the terrace above, where firewood was stacked in a wide arched enclosure.

I heard myself say, "I'll take it. We don't have to go in if your Olive doesn't like visitors."

"You'll *take* it?" he asked, stubbing his toe on a rock put next to the doorway for scraping mud from boots.

"This is it," I said in space.

MacGrath was silent for a minute. "Don't you want to know what's inside?" he said finally.

"How many bedrooms does it have?"

"Well, it has the two. There's the study upstairs. *It* has the view over the trees. In back of the living room there's the terrace built next to the garden. I did tell you the price is eight hundred dollars for the four months starting in May?"

"Okay," I said.

"Are you *quite* sure?" he asked. "I'm getting rather drenched standing here."

I nodded.

"Well, that suits me," said MacGrath, getting back with a grunt into his car.

That following spring my station wagon almost touched the ground under the weight of my suitcases, camera equipment, and a blue-and-gold macaw I inherited along the way, named Arabello, who shrieked whenever the bottom of the car scraped against the pavement. The last part of the road leading to Olive's turnoff was blocked by a small Renault. I got out, managed to pick up the front end of the midget car, and moved it to the edge of the field. The bird, seizing the opportunity of the open car door, flapped its wings wildly and took off through the trees in a blaze of tropical colors and cries. It was a fine beginning.

I remember thinking, as I drove down that road in the South of France, that my work as a photographer had finally paid off. My first book of pictures was about to be published in Paris, and fate had now provided me with a flawless house on the Riviera, I was in my early twenties then, and firmly—unalterably, it seemed—in love, believing (though by nature skeptical) that these might be the most glorious years of my life; believing, too, that time still stretched endlessly ahead of me. As though imitating this, the wide expanse of the Mediterranean reaching all the way to Africa was just over the hills beyond the carefully tended garden.

By the end of the first week I was accustomed to the daily arrivals of the housekeeper, Rose, who appeared each morning with the mandatory *flûte* of bread piercing the air above her shopping basket; accustomed, I should say, to the languorous rhythm of pleasant meals and walks, and summer heat already far enough advanced for us to close the shutters against it at noon. By the second week I had acquired a small motorbike, which I would ride in fast-motion, blurring through the hills down to Cannes. Before the month was over I had visited the same café often enough to achieve the status of an habitué. With his beret, his tobacco-stained *mégot* sending smoke into his squinted eyes (both hands immersed in the soapy waters below the bar, turning the glasses, the cups, clattering the cutlery), the bartender would extend his elbow in an amputee's handshake and ask whether I wanted my usual *pastis*. I was urgently happy. I had been absorbed into the scenery.

The casino in Cannes was very glittery, with fine cars parked in front and fine boats moored out in back, and everyone splendid and rich. I stayed my distance. But one adventurous evening I wandered into the small room where the crowd seemed to be playing only for high stakes. I had been there only long enough to watch all my chips quickly swallowed when I became aware of an Indian gentleman, not particularly well dressed, who was losing, as I watched, almost a quarter of a million dollars. His chips were in large denominations, called plaques, and they were raked across the lawn of baize as casually as my last ten dollars, which went along with them.

I looked with conspicuous bewilderment at the man standing next to me. "He's lost a lot of money," I said. By now a small crowd was around the table.

The man said, "I figure, all told, it's half a million. That's tonight. Last night he lost two hundred thousand."

I approximated a brief gale through my teeth.

"Why don't you go over and talk to him?" he said. "No one talks to him. He just keeps putting down his chips."

I looked again at my partner in this dialogue, a man in his early fifties, tan, too tan, with a face that might have belonged to a politician. His smile, extremely pleasant, had no weight.

"Why don't you?" I said.

"Hell, no," he answered. "I only talk to millionaires when I think I can borrow money from them."

Then he flashed his candidate's smile, and I found myself walking over to the Indian gentleman, who had stopped playing. The others at the table had lost interest in the gambler, nervously clicking his heavy plaques from one hand to the other.

All I could think of to say was "I guess you've had a bad run of luck."

He was a very short man and he looked way up at me with all the sorrows of Asia.

"You're right! You're right!" His clipped voice turned up at its edge. "Last night, too. It's not been a good stay in Cannes, not like last year. My wife will be upset when I get back home to India. She doesn't approve." He simulated a chuckle. "But every year, I must. I must."

"Ah yes, " I said, with sympathy.

"And you?" he was kind enough to ask.

I opened empty hands.

"Maybe you bring me luck?" he asked. "Take a chip and see." And with this he handed me a plaque for what I remember was the equivalent of rent and expenses for the summer.

My hand accepted it, turned over in an arc, and pointed at myself. I said, "Me?"

"Yes, yes," he answered distractedly. "See if you can win something. I would certainly like to win something tonight." Then, once again magnetized by the metal ball spinning round, he edged toward the table and seemed to forget about me.

"Did he do what I thought I saw him do?" exclaimed my politician friend, now crowding next to me.

What happened as I stood with the plaque in my hand was that I then walked over to the Indian gentleman and gave it back. I had not expected to do this, but there it was.

"You gave it back? You gave it *back?*" This from the

politician, who finally introduced himself as Zachary Osborne.

"My first impulse was to cash it in. But I'd regret it later. Anyway, out of principle," I said, defending myself, "if I'm going to lose money, I'm going to lose my own money."

"What about winning, for Christ's sake?" asked Osborne.

"The same goes for winning," I said. "I guess I don't win when I gamble. It's not where I'm lucky."

"You're crazy!" Osborne was genuinely angry. "It's not that difficult to win."

"Hey, how come you're not out there winning?" I asked, now on firmer ground.

Zachary Osborne—Zach to his friends—was a man of fast cars, golf, deals that never quite went through, and considerable charm. He lived on an inherited income and was just about to divorce his fourth wife, suitably a French showgirl specializing in the cancan. Because of the French courts, she had to be photographed *in flagrante* with another man, relieving Osborne of the weight of one more ex-wife's alimony. He had gleefully made the arrangements through a local detective agency. I learned all this quickly, for that evening after the casino we made the rounds of his bars and I was introduced, my back slapped heartily each time, as the guy who gave back a two-thousand-dollar plaque at the casino.

I arrived back on the dirt road leading to the Mas Katia late that night, drunk and disheveled, and found the small Renault parked once again in the middle, blocking my way like a reproach. I got out, pounded on its fender, then tried to move it once again. Instead, I slipped onto the grass next to the road, and alternating between hilarity and anger, I abandoned my car and staggered down the rest of the road, resolving the next morning to seek out its owner.

Since I preferred using my motorbike to the station wagon, the frequently misparked Renault never bothered me very much. Now I realized that there was a narrow overgrown path running from where the car was parked, across the field, and descending into a thicket of trees. That morning I followed the footpath through small clouds of insects and field flowers, from strong sunlight into the darkness of the trees. Set among the low branches was a small stone house I had never noticed before. I knocked on the door and no one answered. Then I peered in through the window at a thinly furnished living room.

All the expatriate's artifacts were there. A day-old copy of the *International Herald Tribune* lay on the coffee table open to the crossword puzzle, which was half finished, as was the glass of red wine next to it. The paperback Simenon was on the armrest of the one good chair, spread open face-down. It was in French. The French dictionary was underneath the reading glasses. There, too, was the package of American cigarettes, the bottle of scotch, the letters with American postmarks—these on the windowsill —the frayed address book, the straw garden hat, the string bag with today's sparse shopping. Whoever lived here was alone in the determined way of someone who might have known the opposite.

"Just a minute, just a minute," I heard coming from some other room. Then quick steps on a wooden staircase, and the doorknob was seized, turned back and forth, a lock jangled, jammed, turned once again, and the door was yanked open.

"Oh!" said the woman. "I was just drying my hair."

I stumbled over an excuse, actually apologizing for peer-

ing through the window. When I remembered the reason
for the visit, I said, "It's just that, well, you're the one with
the Renault, I guess."

"And you're the one who moves it," she said. She was a
pretty woman with white hair and a delicate body. I
learned later that her hair had turned white when she was
nineteen, and the day I stood on her doorstep with my
apologies and recriminations she had just celebrated, by
herself, her fortieth birthday.

"Do you do it alone? I mean, if you move it alone, you
certainly are strong."

"Well, I . . ."

"No matter. Come in. I know it's strange to come in the
front door and find yourself in the kitchen—watch your
head, the ceiling's very low—really, this is a dwarf's house.
I feel like the little woman who lived in the dell, or whatever she was called. How do you do, by the way." She extended her hand. "My name is Caroline Phipps."

"How do you do, Miss Phipps."

"Mrs.," she corrected, blushing in the way of extremely
fair women. A pink rush mottled her skin from her breast-
bone past the curve of her neck to her cheeks.

"Ex-Mrs., actually," she said. "I do pull the car over as
far as I can to the side of the road, but it's so small, a
dwarf's car, really. Its tiny wheels won't go up, up, over the
side of the road because it rises. Of course, if it's *picked*
up and *placed* there . . ."

"I only do that so I can get by, you see, because I've
rented the house farther down the road belonging to a
woman named Olive . . ."

"I hear it's a lovely little house, that one. Oh, my
goodness, the refrigerator door is open. The floor slants,
you see, which is what happens when you rent a house for

only ninety dollars a month. I've already been here almost a year. No wonder nothing stays cold in it. The refrigerator, I mean. The house is always cold."

It was that afternoon that I cleared a space next to the road large enough for Caroline Phipps's car. After the day had cooled, she came over, she said, to pay a call. I had the impression that she had made only a few friends since she lived in France, and was pleased, though timid, about this new opportunity. She refused a drink, refused to sit either inside or on the terrace. All she wanted to do, she said, was see the house, and so she went into its few rooms and out into the garden saying how much she loved houses, loved them more than anything else in the world. She added that her whole life had been spent waiting to have a perfect house of her own. Then she mentioned that she had come to France because she could just about live on the three hundred and seventy-five dollars a month alimony from Mr. Phipps, never intending to go back to America again. With this she stepped back outside into the gathering darkness and walked down the overgrown path.

From that day on I ran into Caroline Phipps frequently, waiting on line in the post office or prodding the bread at the local *boulanger.* Our first encounter at her house seemed to have set us into a similar orbit.

"I must say, it's pleasant running into you," she said one day, with exuberance. "I'm alone so much of the time, I find I've begun talking to myself."

As I tried to form an appropriately polite answer, she added, smiling, "Alone out of choice, I mean."

We were standing on the small town square of La Roquette sur Siagne. Several bands of gypsies had set up their wagons in an empty field just beyond the town, walking into the provincial square to solicit money and food, and read an occasional palm.

Caroline said, "I don't think these gypsies are as romantic as everyone else does. I think a vagabond's life must be miserable. I'd hate it. I'd do anything to stay *put*, in one place. Now, leave me *alone!*" she said, shooing away a pair of small children with hard eyes and hoop earrings. "Goodness, I barely have enough money to take care of myself!"

"Don't you ever go out?" I asked. Now that I had seen her a few times I felt friendly enough to ask.

"In the *evenings?*" she asked.

"Well, yes. I guess that's what I mean."

"What would I do in the *evenings?* You mean, drive into Cannes and sit at a café?"

"Lots of ladies go out at night."

"No," she said cautiously. "I'd rather sit home and read a book."

"At dusk, then," I said. "At dusk you can be completely respectable."

"Well, *dusk*, as you say, is a better idea. But not yet. Not this week."

She got into her small car, waved, and drove away from the square.

The phone at the Mas Katia did not ring often. The easy southern rhythm, as calm as the sea along that coast, was propelling me through the summer without intrusions. The macaw lived unchained on a cerulean-blue hula hoop, swaying in the garden far enough away from the wisteria vines not to prune them with its powerful beak.

When Osborne telephoned, the usually silent phone set Arabello to shrieking, Rose to running, the calm momentarily ruffled. Can I ever piece together such a gentle puzzle again?

"Well, I got her," said Zach enthusiastically. "With a wine steward from a restaurant in St.-Paul. Poor bastard."

"You got who?" I asked. I had just lifted the last leaf from my artichoke at lunch and was preparing to cut away the heart. The lavender growing next to the terrace had that afternoon attracted a large number of bees and one of them had landed in my wine, buzzing on its back. Would I postpone the operation on the artichoke to spare the bee? Would the bee retaliate? These were my problems when the phone rang.

"My *wife!*" he said in triumph. "They took a room at the Negresco. Pretty fancy for a wine steward but I guess he thought it was worth it, though frankly she's never been that good. Anyway, the detectives waited a half hour and then opened up the door and took the picture. I knew if I waited long enough I'd catch her. How do you feel about helping me celebrate? All my other buddies are either out of town or sailing . . ."

From his tone I realized that there were not too many buddies and I invited him over for a drink.

When it was dark, Cannes glowed pink across the olive grove in back of the house, and the garden's night scents hugged close to the earth. Occasionally an owl hooted. The silence subdued Osborne and I realized it was a mistake to have held his celebration there. Now he dwelled on the misfortunes he had experienced in business—he had once owned the Ford dealership for the Great Lakes area—and how each new venture seemed to deprive him of more capital, each new relationship seemed to end in divorce. By the time I realized what was happening, that Osborne

flourished only in a public atmosphere, he had abandoned
the idea of a further celebration and decided instead to
drive to Monte Carlo.

I said, out of the blue, "You ought to meet Caroline."

"Who's Caroline?" asked Osborne.

Then I told him the story about the car blocking the
road and the woman living in the woods. Zachary did not
seem to care much about meeting her, but I hammered
away at what a good idea it was. Hatching a plan as I
went along, I carefully described Caroline, assuring Osborne that without mentioning him, I would urge her into
Cannes on a certain day late in the afternoon, to the terrace of the Carlton Hotel. Then he could buy her a drink
or send one over to her table. By now Osborne was getting
into his car, a silver Porsche. He agreed to the idea without
enthusiasm.

"What else can you tell me about her?" he asked as he
started the powerful motor.

Shouting over the sound, I said, "I've already told you
more than I know."

Caroline drove into Cannes the afternoon I knew Osborne would be sitting on the terrace of the Carlton. I had
joked with her about how timid she was, and so—dressed
in pink and very pretty—she went, she said, to spite me. I
did not tell her about Osborne. I don't know why I had
taken up meddling in anyone's affairs, though it might have
been because I had too much free time, or because I wanted
my lighthearted, lightheaded summer to be contagious. But
maybe it was just because I liked them both and wished
them well.

For several days after she went into Cannes, Caroline's
car was gone from its parking place. When I bicycled into
town I found myself checking the streets for a small

Renault with foreign plates. At certain moments her disappearance was worrying and I thought of calling the police. Then one morning, like a comedy routine, the car was back and next to it was the silver Porsche.

There is a sense of minor triumph in manipulating the lives of others when it seems to work out. I knew when I saw Osborne's car parked on the road that the image was too whimsical, exceeding even the limits I had put on it. I remember passing the two cars on my bike, looking at them in their cheek-to-cheek pose, parked that way, I thought, to make me smile. But beyond the sense of triumph I realized that I had set something in motion without knowing what I was doing, and no matter what happened from then on, part of the responsibility would be mine, tagging along with the caravan like a gypsy's dog. But I managed to forget quickly about this, and by the time we met later that week, there was a lot of laughter and good spirits, and talk about happy times ahead.

The summer was to end that way, in a roseate haze, in perfect harmony with the way it had begun. By the middle of September I had to go back to work in Rome. I traded in my small station wagon for a small sports car, which I took for trial runs along the Moyen and Grand Corniches as the weather turned chilly and the beach clubs began to shut down. Caroline and Zachary decided to leave together for Marbella, where someone had promised them a villa, and they drove away, past the small path leading to the house in the woods. Although many of the flowers were still blossoming, the fields had been scorched by the summer sun.

They drove as far as St.-Tropez and then called me to meet them there for dinner. Any excuse would get me back in my new car and I drove there through the wind-

ing roads—there was no highway then—speeding past the
pine forests, the rich earth of the Esterel the same color as
the late-afternoon sky. And so we said goodbye once again
with the harbor of St.-Tropez in the background.

Their story would end there, as would mine, if none of
us had grown any older.

But although I have lost many of my essential documents, contracts, leases, and such, I have kept address
books of the last two decades and I counted the listings for
the Osbornes, which is what they came to be called. Since
the day they drove down the road leading away from the
Mas Katia, I have fourteen entries for them.

The South of France, the coast of Spain, Portugal above
Lisbon, Corfu, back to the South of France, Rome, back
again to the Riviera. They tacked across the watering
places of the sixties and seventies like frantic sailboats.
They were not alone in these journeys, crisscrossing with
others who moved at various speeds through the same
waters of the Mediterranean, still the corner of the world
that tugs most often at the foreigners and promises them
something connected to the past. They were decent people, the Osbornes, and if somewhere along the way I realized that each of them drank too much, that the whole
bunch of watering-place foreigners drank too much and
acted like partygoers left over from the frivolity of the
twenties and thirties (forgetting that the time for all that
aimlessness had long since passed and was scorned), my
affection for them remained intact.

It was while I was staying briefly on the Cap d'Antibes,
about six years later, that I saw them again. They had
moved back to Cannes. Zachary had tried without success
to become the agent of a French wine company in Madrid,
and he spent and lost a lot of money attempting it. They

were pleased to be back in Cannes, which they tried to think of as their home. In the hills near Opio, they had rented a small house with a rock garden, which Caroline began to fill with carefully tended plants. They also acquired a Dalmatian puppy and several pieces of furniture from the local dealers in *brocante*. Caroline said once again, when I called them, that she did not want to be a vagabond any longer, that she intended to stay there the rest of her life. The first time I saw them they seemed very happy.

Caroline's appearance had changed. Throughout that first summer we met, I had come to realize how young she was, that the prematurely white hair had acted as a costume to give the impression of age and worldliness not in keeping with either her character or her real age. Now the disharmony had almost vanished and she was quickly becoming what she had seemed then to be, a middle-aged American woman who had lived in many places, searching always for the right one.

I saw that everything was not right between them when, at dinner at my friend's villa in the Cap d'Antibes, Caroline mentioned too often how Zachary was always failing at everything. I suspected that the word *failing* had come up a good deal by the way his hand tightened around the wineglass, his knuckles suddenly white. Then something in Caroline's next sentence coincided with the snap of the broken stem. The wineglass wriggled free from Zachary's unclenched hand, and at the same instant widening tributaries of blood began to cross his palm.

Caroline said, "That was a stupid thing to do," and abruptly left the table to return with a cloth.

Zachary said nothing at all and looked on with detachment while she removed the last sliver of glass with a pair of tweezers. But by the time they got back in the car he was too drunk to drive. Miming apologies, Caroline took the wheel and they were gone.

I saw them only once again before I left the Riviera, when we went to the Galerie Maehgt in St.-Paul-de-Vence. Traffic snaked along, infecting all the roads leading to the coast, and we drove in a steady line past the all-new condominiums now covering the landscape. We made the mistake of looking through the stone arch leading to the town of St.-Paul-de-Vence, the classic ex-rustic hill town of Provence, now polished up, adorable, annulled. Separately, we pondered those pressing matters, Change and Loss, and now inside the museum we went our own ways, weaving in and out of its desolate landscape like zombies. Caroline appeared next to a wide window, Zachary's silhouette briefly materialized from behind a large steel sculpture, disappearing again behind a block of poured concrete. I, too, must have been concealed and then revealed by black monuments of Abstract Expressionism. By the time I met up with Caroline near a refreshment booth, we were both filled with a nameless anxiety. Zachary was nowhere to be found.

Caroline said nervously, "He's probably in the car. He keeps a flask in the car."

"I wouldn't mind a drink, either," I said.

"He's turning into an alcoholic . . ." she began.

"Listen," I said, interrupting, "if you keep nagging at him, he won't have any choice."

"We're turning sour. I can feel it but I can't stop it."

"If you were both fish," I said, "I'd change the water in your tank."

"I don't know what to do."

"Why don't you try going your own ways?"

"That's the most ridiculous thing I've ever heard," said Caroline, her face flushed. "How can I leave him in the state he's in?"

"That's a great line," I said. "It's been responsible for most of the world's unhappiness."

"You used to be more sympathetic."

I looked at her and remembered how she had put on her good dress to drive into Cannes at dusk to the terrace of the Carlton, where Zachary would buy her a drink.

Throughout the next years, we corresponded; occasionally we spoke on the phone. The year I decided to leave Europe, Caroline and Zachary appeared in Rome and asked me to help them find an apartment quickly, they said, because they were fearful of staying in a hotel. This was because Zachary had some problems with the authorities in France over bad checks he had been given and, in turn, written, and he was now on the list at Interpol, required to register at the police station within a day or two after entering Italy.

My mother, too, was in Rome that year, and she was married at the Campidoglio. I have a photograph of all of us, including the Osbornes, standing around the magistrate, who sits in a gilded chair. Several months later, Caroline and Zachary decided to marry officially in the same place, and I have another photograph similarly composed, with many of the same faces, the same postures, the same clothing, and the magistrate in both pictures wears the same expression of profound skepticism.

It was during that period in Rome, the beginning of the seventies, that Zachary lost most of the rest of his money backing a movie which was never finished. But he suddenly stopped drinking and it seemed as though it might

be the last of his failures. Sometime after that, he returned
to States, alone. He wrote telling me he found a job with a
computer company in Texas because his money had all
run out, and his salary as a trainee was two hundred dollars
a week. This was quite a switch, he wrote, from the old
days in Cannes when he drove a silver Porsche and went to
the casino. He now had a new girlfriend, half his age and
very pretty, and they were thinking maybe of getting
married. He did not mention Caroline. It must have been
that same year when I heard from Caroline that she was
living in the South of France, that she and Zachary had
divorced and her alimony was about what it had been
fifteen years before, when she left her Renault parked in
the middle of our road. Now, she wrote, she was living by
herself once again. I doubted that I would see her for a
long while.

And yet, and yet: there I was again, car piled high with
my foreigner's lot, dog next to me in the front seat, both
of us leaning first north then south as we curved along the
autoroute from Milan to Genoa and on to France through
the long haze-filled tunnels, past the indifferent, unseeing
customs. No one cared about investigating us: my dog,
India, could have been an elephant, the suitcases could
have been stacked with gold. We were waved cheerfully
out of Italy, waved cautiously into France. With the tricolor snapping triumphantly in the wind, the sea on the
left, we exulted in the still, soft air even though it was December, even though the sun was no longer shining and
the air had lost its fragrance, even though we were no
longer young.

Gaunt rock stars streamed by along the autoroute in
their brand-new Rolls-Royces, while, still, peasant ladies

hacked at olive wood, and cabbages grew in small stunted gardens, squeezed in between the brash villas untouched by age or use. Men with sticks hobbled across the highway with no other way to get to its other side; crossing, it seemed, from one abandoned farmhouse to another. Between Nice and the Cap d'Antibes three pyramids had risen, far larger than Egypt's: colossal, banded with windows and balconies. In Juan-les-Pins, I turned off to the old road, once again passing the Château de l'Horizon, now down at heel and for sale. I did not think to glance up at the hill where the Villa Cleopatra had once been. Now I was once again in France, once again knocking at its unyielding door.

I settled into my small rented house just above Cannes. Beyond my desk, past an avalanche of rooftops, was the sea. My small garden, overgrown with weeds and wildflowers, had the requisite orange tree, cactus, olive, and rosemary bush. With neighbors on all sides, the cypress trees, pressed close, managed to give me the impression that I was almost secluded. The house was comfortable: three rooms in a row and a view of the sea, and I was grateful.

Everything had changed, nothing had changed. My first hesitant forays into town were attempts to make peace with the present and not let the past interfere too much, not be bothered that the café I knew was no longer where it had been, that the cheese shop had given way to a jewelry store. No time for complaints about the present, no room to incorporate too much nostalgia. We live in the moment or we are left struggling like hooked fish, our gills straining for the element we once knew, for what once had sustained us. If you come to see me and tell me too often what once has been, I will turn you out.

In town I had not forgotten the interdictions posted everywhere, and they had sprouted, spread. This passionate interest in reproach and denial seemed, even in the present, to hold the country together. How could I keep from smiling? France had remained intact.

When I telephoned Caroline, her voice trilled on the phone. Still there, still a survivor. Will we all end up back here? she wondered in a rush of nervous laughter. Then she invited me to dinner.

I found her relatively unchanged. Perhaps she had gained a bit of weight, but it suited her, kept her from seeming too frail. There was an almost masculine matter-of-factness about her: she was who she was. Her white hair was now cropped short. No vanity seemed to obscure her. We looked at each other with some awkwardness.

"Time," she said. "I don't know what we would say to each other if we were meeting for the first time. I think we wouldn't even say anything beyond hello. Then we'd go on to speak to someone else. Our lives have turned out in such different ways. And now we seem generations apart. I guess we always have."

"Hardly," I said, not quite believing it.

"Nothing has turned out the way I had hoped. Isn't it strange? I'm still without a house of my own."

I said, "I never should have persuaded you to have that drink in Cannes . . ."

She did not disagree. There was a long, steady silence. Then we brightened because it was too disgusting to sit there and mull over past scenes and wrong turns and injustices. Over her third Bourbon she told me that Zach had stopped sending money about a year after their divorce, that he had married once again. Their divorce had come

about because each of them realized when finally he quit
drinking that they had been as much held together by alcohol as separated by it. Her own savings were almost all
spent and she did not know how much longer she could
stay in the small apartment she had found.

I recognized some of the objects and furniture in her
living room from earlier times. She had laid a fire, and sitting near its warmth was a black cat and the Dalmatian I
remembered as a puppy when they had lived in Opio. On
the radio the government station was playing Schubert's
Third Impromptu, the melancholy strands of piano music
filling our silence.

"Why don't you leave, Caroline," I said. "Leave before
you have to let all this go piece by piece."

"Back to America? Oh, but I couldn't. I wouldn't know
where to begin. I've lived in Europe too long. It's too late!
What would they want with a white-haired woman almost
sixty? If I went back there, all this would have added up
to nothing. I might as well not have bothered coming in
the first place!" The words came out too quickly.

"I'm sorry," I said. "I'm deeply sorry. I don't know why
I seem to say this to my friends when they seem so . . ."

"It's not that I'm unhappy! I've been taking care of an
elderly couple. I read to them and take them for walks.
They're Americans and they're really terribly old, in their
late eighties. Imagine! They've been here since the time of
the Fitzgeralds. They've seen it all happen, seen it all fall
apart. And they've told me they will leave me a small income providing I look after them till the end of their days.
I'll be taken care of, don't you see? Then I can stay in
France or move back to Italy, or even go to Greece, where
it's cheaper, so I'm told. If I'm careful I can just manage to

keep going. I still have a few of my father's first editions
of Blake I can sell."

I put down my drink, looked at the fire and the two
peaceful animals, listened to the last elegant notes of the
Schubert, and all at once I wanted to walk out of the door,
I wanted not to know—for one of the few times in my life
—how the story would end, because I knew that it would
be a bad end and that I was looking at and listening to an
atmosphere so doomed that it might perish before my eyes
if I stayed around. The cat now stretched, lazily applying
a paw to its cheek, graced with an animal's unconcern
with what awaited it, paying no mind to the woman who
sat in the poorly upholstered velvet chair explaining again
and again to the air around her why she wanted to stay in
Europe.

There was no stopping her. "Everyone's leaving," she
said in a rush. "I realize that no one comes to Europe to
live anymore. It's all finished, and I mean *all* of it. Now it's
the other way around. *They* have become *us!* They want
everything we escaped from. Time is money in Europe,
just as it is for us back home. But I want to stay anyway,
because it's too late for me to change. Maybe it will all
come around again, just like it was in the old times. I've
gambled my life on it, you see, like riding a horse to the
end of the universe. I can't get off unless I'm thrown from
it. When I first came here"—she gestured through invisible
walls to the South of France—"it was like taking a lover, a
lover for the rest of my life. Maybe I came at the wrong
time, maybe it was all through before I even got here. But
I can't leave it and go back to America, where I'll be just
another lonely woman pushing a cart in the supermarket,
weeping among the groceries, with Muzak piped into the
background, living in a one-room studio, hoping to get a

part-time job. Another woman nobody notices. But here, I'm Caroline-who-lives-in-Europe! They take me to dinner when they come through and tell me how lucky I am. I really can't explain . . ."

"You've explained, Caroline," I said.

I try to think of whether it was my impatience with her or the fact that I was alarmed by the bleakness surrounding Caroline that kept me from seeing much of her those winter months. I knew we were no longer close enough for me to affect her. Also, I was trying very hard on my own to maintain an optimistic stance, trying not to think about how everything had changed with Europe and America, trying, too, not to think about money. It was something I had to overcome each day, like ignoring an ever-present arthritis: ignore the astonishing price of a hotel tonight, the price of dinner, of gasoline, of the highway tolls.

I drove everywhere along the coast. A good American friend visiting me had developed a surreal antidote to our money anxieties, and we tried it out in St.-Tropez along the same quay that witnessed my goodbye to the Riviera and the Osbornes so long ago. There was an outdoor phone booth. We wedged into it, put a five-franc piece into the toll box, dialed twelve numbers, and reached, miraculously, the United States of America. Five francs—one dollar—bought us thirty seconds.

"Did I wake you? I thought you would like to know I'm in St.-Tropez, at the harbor, and . . . What? Yes, it's really me. Yes, I'm in France. As I was saying, I'm in St.-Tropez. It's noon. I'm about to have a glass of white wine. I was thinking of you, so I thought I'd call." Click.

We took turns at this game, leaving the booth for some

wine, returning to it less sober, with some new inspiration, some new friend in mind. The idea was that when you stepped out of the phone booth it no longer mattered that the few fishermen held their lines in the water with no hope because the Mediterranean there was polluted, that most of the people along the quay were tourists with cameras, fingering the fishnets, and that if you did sit at a café for a few glasses of wine you might not manage to pay for your lunch too. What mattered was the illusion that you had given your friend at the other end of the line, and given to yourself as well, for only a dollar, that everything was fine, just fine.

By the time winter was over I realized that more than a month had gone by without talking to Caroline. I had been in Paris for a while, and just when I drove up to my house in Cannes, Caroline was ringing my doorbell.

She said at a clip, "I ought to tell you that I'm selling everything. I've put an ad in the newspaper. I've been calling you all this last week to get your advice but I've decided anyway. I've got to leave. Those elderly people who promised to leave me some money if I keep taking care of them will never die. Never! They will keep going if only out of spite. To spite the Riviera. Whenever I read to them or take them for walks they reminisce about what it was once like when Russian princes owned villas and there were Dusenbergs driving along the Grand Corniche. And then I take my small salary and drive back home to go to the supermarket in Cannes. I don't bother any longer with the little *épicier*, the little *boulanger*, the *quincaillerie*, all those names I was once so thrilled to learn. Now I stand on line with my shopping cart and I might as well be back in South Bend, Indiana."

I put my key into the front door and looked back at the

Mediterranean. How could it not have been painful to leave it behind? My dog, India, rushed into the living room ahead of us.

"And the animals?" I asked.

"I don't want to talk about them."

I said sharply, "You've got to take them with you. After all this time you can't leave them here in France."

"Look," she said with feigned patience. "The dog is twelve years old. I can't cart him back to America and drag him from hotel room to hotel room. I can't even manage myself. No one wants him. I've asked all around. And about the cat, well, my feeling is that cats survive. They never become really attached—they're sort of halfway between a dog and a plant, if you see what I mean—I'll leave the window open so it can come and go. I was hoping that my friends would feed it every now and then. I can't *afford* to be too sentimental! The only way I can get through this is by not being sentimental. I don't even know what I'll do when I get back to America. I'm terrified!"

"Why are you so terrified?" I said angrily. "Why does everyone who has to go back home behave like a patient being dragged off to an institution?"

"What about you?" she asked, flushed pink with indignation. "What would you say if you'd been living here all this time and you had to leave?"

"I'd say, goodbye Europe. See you again some other time."

"You would *not!* A friend of mine had to leave France last autumn. She couldn't afford to live here anymore. But she really had no place to go, no *fantasies*, because Europe, you see, was always the fantasy. So she got on the plane, settled herself in her seat, and told the stewardess not to disturb her until they landed. Then she opened her pill box and took all the pills. They thought she was still sleeping when the plane got to New York. But, of course, it was too late."

Spring arrived. Heading for the seacoast, the Germans were the first to arrive, then the Belgians, the Dutch, and the Swiss. They all came funneling down from the darkness and cold of the north in their mad dash to the sea. There was barely time to put the finishing touches on the Riviera.

I guess I avoided visiting Caroline because among other things I could not look her dog in the face, nor could I find a home for it. And so spring advanced, and whenever I thought about Caroline I thought about the approaching casualty of her dog. Maybe she knew this, because when she called to say goodbye she said that she was now alone.

I remember only two things Caroline said that last time I went to see her. I found her sitting alone in her apartment. Everything was gone but the one worn chair. Her feet were propped up on a carton and there was a cane leaning against her chair, because she had sprained her ankle while taking her household apart. Everything had been sold but the chair. On the walls, the marks of the pictures had remained, and half of a pair of curtains fluttered next to an open window.

She said, "I was just thinking: where do the young people dream of going, if not to France?" Then she took her cane and knocked it in anger against the tile floor. In the afternoon light, holding the cane firmly in her hand, she looked gothic.

And then, without turning to me, she added, "You know something? Something extraordinary? In all this time I never really learned to speak French."

The April mimosa was everywhere, scrambling up and down the hills, along the highways; it decorated the floats of the Mimosa Parade. Thrown to the spectators like confetti, it blanketed the Croisette and the streets surrounding it.

I drove through the yellow streets and thickening traffic, took the keys from under Caroline's mat, and let myself into the empty house. Its dampness struck me, its echoing sounds and lifelessness. As I was looking for a bowl for the cat food the doorbell rang.

"I've brought some prospective tenants," said a well-dressed Frenchwoman in the cooing voice reserved for strangers.

A young French couple followed on her heels. They circled the two rooms and the kitchen, their noses crinkling.

The husband asked, "Is there a cat here?"

I began to say that there was, that it badly needed a home, but then, because I have lived a certain amount of time and learned that it is frequently better to wait for more information, I pretended not to understand.

"I have a horror of cats," said the wife.

"There is no cat," said the agent. "There might have been a cat once but there is not a cat now. It might have belonged to the woman who lived here."

"I *thought* it was a woman," said the wife. "I don't know why, but I thought it was a woman who lived here. Did she *die* in these rooms? I had a suspicion a woman lived here, and *died* in the bedroom."

"It was a man," I said, though I don't know why.

"It was not a man," the agent cut in. "I happen to know it was a young couple, just the same as these two young people. The husband," she concluded with authority, "was transferred to Nîmes."

"Aha!" said the husband. "Nîmes is a nice town but it is too small, too provincial. You cannot make enough money in Nîmes."

I left, and as I was getting into my car the trio came out of the door, crossed the street, got into another car, and drove away. When I went back into the apartment I found the cat's dish and filled it with the food I had brought. The cat appeared at the open window but would not come in while I was there. I put out my hand to stroke its black coat and it moved away into the overgrown garden. When I spoke, my voice seemed in the emptiness to echo.

I said to it, "You'd better find yourself another home." Then I left and went outside.

The cat came running along the side of the house as soon as I closed the door, expecting, I suppose, that I had gone. It ran swiftly, like a wildcat, its feet barely touching the ground, bounding up onto the ledge to come into the house through the open window. I watched it from the glass door as it stepped carefully across the room on light feet, the Blackamoor in *Der Rosenkavalier* returning to retrieve the fallen handkerchief. It bounded past the few empty boxes on its way to the kitchen and when it found its dish it ate hungrily, without stopping. Then, barely hesitating, it leaped onto the windowsill to stretch out in the small band of sunlight that promised to grow warmer as the day advanced. Unperturbed about the next day, it lazily licked its paws, fanning them out so that each claw shone.

I hear from Caroline from time to time, and for a while she had found a job as part-time receptionist in a doctor's office near Chicago. She seemed to have made her peace with America; seemed to, I say, because the other day she called me in New York to say that she was going back.

"Do you remember that elderly couple I'd spoken about who wanted me to take care of them till the end of their days? Well, the husband just died, at ninety, and the wife wrote asking me to come over to be her companion."

"So you're going?"

"I'm going back!" she said triumphantly. "Remember I told you that when I went to France it was like taking a lover? Hello? hello, are you still there?"

"Yes, I'm here."

"There was such a long silence, I thought maybe I was speaking into the void." She continued, "It was for life, you see. Maybe I'll never know any other kind of love, ever. So I'm going back to the South of France again. Don't you think that . . . are you there?" Her voice quavered.

I said, "Of course I'm there, Caroline. I've always been there. From the beginning."

"Oh, I wish you could understand, I wish you were here in the same room so you could look at me and see that I mean it, that I am almost trembling, I am so—I don't know how to say it—so much on the threshold. Isn't it all— Europe, I mean—well, my destiny? Don't you . . ."

But I could not answer, for at that instant the phone went dead. And before I called her back I thought, then, that the French would not care about her destiny, going on about their business as before, that the wide, dark ocean she must cross and the flourishing hills rising out of the Mediterranean would not care, indifferent to a random figure returning to seek something she could not name, and that maybe she had reached only the spinning emptiness of the sky that sent a swift thrust to interrupt her in her question, leaving it all unanswered. And when she finally arrived there with all the fragments of past hopes held so delicately and desperately in place, she might be sustained by those shores after all.